THE CADEN CHRONICLES
SKULL CREEK STAKEOUT

Also by Eddie Jones

The Caden Chronicles

Dead Man's Hand (Book 1)

Skull Creek Stakeout (Book 2)

The Curse of Captain LaFoote

*My Father's Business: 30 Inspirational Stories
for Discerning and Doing God's Will*

THE CADEN CHRONICLES

SKULL CREEK STAKEOUT

BOOK TWO

EDDIE JONES

ZONDER**kidz**

ZONDERKIDZ

Skull Creek Stakeout

Copyright © 2013 by Eddie Jones

This title is also available as a Zondervan ebook.

Visit www.zondervan.com/ebooks

Requests for information should be addressed to:

Zonderkidz, 5300 Patterson Ave. SE, Grand Rapids, Michigan 49530

Library of Congress Cataloging-in-Publication Data

Jones, Eddie, 1957 –
    Skull Creek stakeout / Eddie Jones.
        pages cm. – (The Caden chronicles; bk. 2)
        Summary: Fourteen-year-old Nick gets a job as a roving reporter for The Cool Ghoul Gazette, a website on paranormal disturbances, and, on his first assignment, finds a corpse with fangs, bite marks, and a gaping hole in its chest, courtesy of a wooden stake.
        ISBN 978-0-310-72390-5 (softcover)
        [1. Supernatural–Fiction. 2. Reporters and reporting–Fiction. 3. Vampires–Fiction. 4. Web sites–Fiction. 5. Mystery and detective stories.] I. Title.
PZ7.J68534Sku 2013
[Fic]–dc23   2013009460

Published in association with Hartline Literary Agency, Pittsburgh, Pennsylvania 15235.

Zonderkidz is a trademark of Zondervan.

Cover design: Sammy Yuen
Editor: Kim Childress
Illustrations: Owen Richardson
Interior design: Sarah Molegraaf
Interior composition: Greg Johnson/Textbook Perfect

Printed in the United States of America

13 14 15 16 17 18 19 /DCI/ 20 19 18 17 16 15 14 13 12 11 10 9 8 7 6 5 4 3 2 1

I've waited all my life to dedicate a book to Mom and now I can without fear of retribution. Assuming, of course, she can't curse me from the grave. One thing about Mom, you always knew what she was thinking—whether you wanted to know or not. You also knew you were loved.

A year or so ago Mom was on her way to the hairdresser when another driver ran a stop sign and smashed into her Buick. Mom got out, inspected the damage, and exchanged insurance information with the other driver. While waiting for the police to arrive, Mom popped the trunk and motioned the other woman to the rear of her LeSabre.

"My son's a writer," Mom announced, "and I've got some of his books. Do you want a copy?" I wasn't at the crash site, but knowing Mom, I imagine the inflection in her voice and order of words was probably more like: "You do want a copy of my son's book, right?" I'm almost certain of this because the woman bought one copy of my book and a church recipe book. I bet the woman doesn't even cook or have kids.

But that was Mom. Always hawking my books and asking me how my writing was going. She worried constantly I wouldn't make enough as a writer to support my family. I kept telling her our daily provision is God's business; mine was to be obedient and write stories that reflect His truths.

Last year I lost my biggest fan and best salesperson, but God gained a worthy assistant for the running of His kingdom. I can't imagine how God thinks He'll remain in charge now.

The last thing Mom told me was, "I'm not as young as I used to be, son. You need to think about your old mom once in a while and come see me."

I will, Mom. Someday I will.

If you're blessed enough to still have your mom around, give her a hug and whisper, "Love you, Mom." Trust me, it's the best and cheapest gift there is.

Love you, Mom. I miss you.

—EJ

CONTENTS

CHAPTER ONE
A CASE I CAN SINK MY TEETH INTO

Death found me on a hot June morning in Walt Disney World's Tower of Terror.

Minutes before I heard about the vampire in Transylvania, North Carolina, I pulled the seat belt across my waist and showed my hands to the bellhop. Behind me buckles snapped shut; arms shot up. The smiling service attendant in his maroon and gold cap bid us a pleasant stay at the Hollywood Hotel and retreated into the boiler room. Service doors sealed us inside, and the elevator yanked us up.

The young boy seated next to me whispered to his mom, "Why did he make us raise our hands?"

"So when they snap our picture it looks like we're having fun."

"And to prove you're not holding anything in your hand," I offered. "See, if you place a penny on your palm, like this, when the car drops the coin will—"

"Don't you dare try that, Grayson!"

I shoved the penny back in my pocket and said under my breath, "Wasn't suggesting he do it. Just saying that's why they make you put your hands up."

The car stopped on the thirteenth floor. Doors opened. Our elevator car rumbled down a darkened hallway, and the theme song from the *Twilight Zone* began playing through headrest speakers. A short ways in front, Rod Serling magically appeared, warning riders: "You unlock this door with the key of imagination. Beyond it is another dimension—a dimension of sound, a dimension of sight, a dimension of mind. You're moving into a land of both shadow and substance, of things and ideas. You've just crossed over into ... *(dramatic pause)* ... the Twilight Zone."

Instantly a barrage of objects shot past—a wooden door, Einstein's formula for relativity, an eyeball. Windowpanes shattered and shards of glass morphed into twinkling stars. Through the speakers a little girl began singing, "It's raining, it's pouring ..."

Buried in my front pocket, my smartphone began vibrating.

I pulled it out and quickly read the text message. "PHONE ME NOW. RIGHT NOW! GOT KILLER OF A STORY FOR YOU!" It was from Calvin.

Right, I thought. *Bet it's just another zombie fest or supposed house haunting.*

See, weeks earlier I'd signed on to be a reporter for the *Cool Ghoul Gazette* — a website dedicated to exploring ghosts, zombies, werewolves, vampires, and all things supernatural and freaky. For months my parents had been after me to get a summer job. Mom thought I needed to start saving for college, even though I don't start high school until next year. Dad kept saying it was time I did something other than sit around and watch TV, even though watching TV *is* my job.

No kidding. Watching television (online, mostly) is my job. I'm a founding member of TV Cyber Sleuths, a group of teens that analyzes and catalogues crime, cop, and detective shows. We have a huge database of episodes going back almost thirty years, and we use this information to catch real murderers. At least, when law enforcement officials will let us help. Our little group has an 80 percent close rate. That means in most cases we can correctly identify the killer *before* the real detectives can. Problem is, TV Crime Watchers doesn't pay, and making money is apparently a big deal.

"Can't pay for the good life without a good job," Dad keeps reminding me. "And sometimes, you can't even pay for it then."

Dad hoped I'd get a job cutting grass like my cousin Fred. Fred has like a gazillion customers and last summer he made enough to buy his own truck—a used Ford Ranger that has over a hundred thousand miles on it and leaks oil like a Gulf oil well.

But I'm not Fred.

The elevator car stopped. Another set of doors opened, this time revealing a bird's-eye view of Walt Disney World's Hollywood Studios theme park. Crowds choked Sunset Boulevard and moved in random directions like energetic ants bent on beating the other ants to the top of the hill. Children lined up near a pretzel stand to get Buzz Lightyear's autograph. Parents milled about in the designated stroller area.

Our car dropped. Girls screamed; moms shrieked.

Not me. You couldn't have blasted the smile off my face with a power washer. Down we plummeted! Sudden stop, then rocket back up. Once more doors peeled open, and the park flashed before us. Again we fell. Up and down we went with cables yanking us both directions. I'd learned about the cables from watching the Discovery Channel. It seems the initial design of the tower proved too tame. The head of the design team complained that if his tie didn't fly up and hit him in the face, the car wasn't falling fast enough. So they added cables underneath the car, and now when you fall the cable jerks you down at a rate of almost two g's. It's way better than just jumping off a building.

Our car fell the final time, then slowed. Doors opened. Buckles unsnapped. Passengers rushed across the lobby of the old hotel toward the photo counter to see themselves on video monitors.

I checked the floorboard for my phone.

"I think you're looking for this," said Grayson's mom, thrusting my phone at me. "It nearly hit me in the face."

"I'm sorry. I meant to—"

"This is no place for a prank like that. Someone could get hurt."

"I know. I'm really, really sorry."

Grayson's mom, having loudly made her point in front of the other riders, turned away and marched toward the monitors, pulling Grayson along.

I hung back, waited for the crowd to thin, aimed my phone at the monitor, and snapped a picture of the picture of myself. Outside I found Mom and Dad and Wendy waiting for me at the Fast Past gate.

Dad said, "Well? How was it?"

"Awesome! Can I go again?"

"Maybe after lunch," Mom said. "If we have time. We're supposed to be at the ESPN Sports Complex by four."

"She has to be there," I said, cutting my eyes toward Wendy. "Not me."

"We're *all* going," Mom countered. "Your sister's cheerleading is a big deal, and we're going to be there for her."

"Yeah," said Wendy, mounting her virtual high horse. "For once we're doing something *I* want to do."

What do you mean "for once"? I wanted to scream. *That's all we ever do.*

"Speaking of being on time," Dad interrupted, "we'd better start walking. We have lunch reservations at the Brown Derby."

The hostess met us at the door, took our names, and told us to wait. I slid open the keyboard on my phone and caught Mom looking over. I knew what she was thinking — *Family bonding time, and that means no phone* — but Dad was already checking out baseball highlights on *his* smartphone, and Wendy had wandered over to another group of cheerleaders seated at a round table.

"Put it away," Mom said.

The hostess returned and ushered us across the dining room to a window table, dealing each of us a menu. As soon as I looked at the prices, I knew Mom and Dad were wondering how they were going to get out of there for under a hundred dollars. Going to the Brown Derby had been Wendy's idea. She didn't want the other girls on her cheerleading team to know how broke we were, even though I was pretty sure they all knew anyway.

The waiter arrived with a pitcher of water, four glasses, and a friendly smile suggesting he expected a larger tip than he would receive. He started explaining the lunch specials when I interrupted.

"I'm thinking of getting a bowl of lobster bisque."

Dad glanced over. "You sure, son? That doesn't sound like enough for you."

"That last ride left me feeling a little queasy. Just a bowl of soup," I told the waiter. "And maybe some rolls."

Mom closed her menu and said to Wendy, "In that case, how about the two of us split a Cobb salad?"

"But I wanted to get the Noodle Bowl."

"You should eat something light, honey. Remember how your nerves are before you perform."

Dad handed his menu to the waiter. "I'll have the crab cakes."

"As an appetizer?" the waiter asked.

"Make it my meal. We're in sort of a hurry."

"Frank, for goodness' sake. Get the rib eye."

"Saving the steak for later when we celebrate," he said, kissing my sister on top of her head.

The waiter — still smiling but now probably thinking what a bunch of cheapskates we were — closed his order pad and hurried off. While Wendy scanned the restaurant for other girls in the US Spirit Nationals, I told Mom and Dad about the message from my editor, leaving out the part about how my phone went airborne.

"You mean that blogging website?" Mom asked. "That's not a job."

"Sure it is, Mom. A writer in Seattle made almost a grand last month reporting on a zombie festival."

"How much have *you* made?" Wendy asked.

"My story on grave robbers in New Orleans got me seventy-five bucks. The editor has me writing fictional obits and some of the 'Breaking Noose' headlines."

"Did you say *noose*?"

"It's a play on words, Mom. Supposed to be funny."

Our waiter returned with rolls. Dad lathered one with butter and said, "Tell me again how you get paid. By the number of visitors to the site?"

"Not to the site, Dad. To my article. See, each reporter is responsible for coming up with his or her own story. I can write on any topic as long as it deals with the supernatural. Once it goes live, I share the post with friends, get them to click on the link, comment on the story, and spread the word."

Mom said, "Sounds like a scam."

"At first I thought it might be. But then my editor sent me a screen grab of some of the royalty payments. Anytime I get a thousand visits to my article, I earn like five dollars. If I do a good job and have the right key phrases and words in the article, it can go viral."

"That means the story becomes popular," Wendy explained to Mom and Dad. "For those not familiar with the modern technological world. So, Nick, are you saying you actually got some hits? I'm mildly impressed."

"My pay is all based on how many eyeballs I can pull," I said.

"Eyeballs?"

"Readers, Dad. We've got this cool eyeball counter on the bottom of each story that shows how popular an article is. Ghost sightings are big right now. I think that's why the site's owner wanted me on his staff. My name lends credibility to the site."

Mom displayed a frosty look of skepticism. "You mean because of what happened in Deadwood? That wasn't a ghost story."

"But it was a ghost town. And I caught the killer."

"Who threatened to kill you, I might add."

"Fact is, I'm a pretty good writer, Mom. At least that's what I've been told."

"Well, if you ask me," Wendy chimed in, "the *Cool Ghoul Gazette* still has a credibility problem if they're letting you write for them."

Before I could respond with a snarky comment, my phone buzzed.

I looked at Mom and said, "Speaking of the *Cool Ghoul* ..."

"Not while we're eating."

"But we're not, yet." I pivoted in my chair and answered the call. "Can't talk right now, Calvin. I'm eating lunch with my family."

"But I have a really sick story for you."

I saw Mom scowling at me. "Let me call you back after I'm done eating."

"In Transylvania."

"Like in Romania?"

"North Carolina."

"Shut up. There's really a town called that?" I asked.

Out of the corner of my eye I saw Mom mouthing, "Hang up right now."

"Outside of Asheville," Calvin was saying. "Get this. Oh, this is so good." I could hear Calvin's excitement through the phone. "They found the victim with a wooden stake in his chest."

"I gotta go. I'll call you when I'm done eating."

"Did you hear what I said, bro? The dead guy is a vampire!"

Just then our waiter arrived, which distracted Mom for a few seconds.

I said to Calvin, "Bet it's just another mannequin stuck in a cornfield dressed to look like Edward Cullen."

"Come on, dude. This is huge!"

"Has to be a hoax. No way there's a real live vampire in Transylvania, North Carolina."

"Won't know for sure until you check it out. They found the body yesterday on the golf course at a place called the Last Resort. How creepy is that? Today's Wednesday so I need you on this right away."

"I told you already. I'm in Florida with my family. My sister has her middle school cheerleading competition tonight."

"Think of all the hits this story is going to get," Calvin continued. "Assuming we report it first."

"Come on, seriously? You really think the victim is a vampire?"

"Who cares what I think? It's the perfect *Cool Ghoul* story! One our readers can sink their teeth into. Hey! Let's go with that as the title."

I groaned audibly.

"So whaddya say, bro? You want the story or don't you?"

"I'll call you back." I hung up on Calvin and looked at Mom. "What?"

Dad got that serious look on his face the way he does sometimes when he's about to say something he thinks is really important. "Did I hear right? The owner of the publication wants you to cover a story in North Carolina?"

"Editor. The owner of the site is a graduate student at Yale. Don't worry, though. I'm not going. Mom's right. I'd hate to miss a chance to watch Wendy blow her big debut as flyer."

"Jerk."

"Love you too, sis."

"What's a flyer?" Dad asked.

"Seriously, Dad? You don't know my position?"

"Flyer is the girl at the top of the pyramid," I whispered to Dad.

"I knew that."

"Then it's settled," Mom said. "Nick's staying. Now can we eat before our food gets cold?"

"Hold on a second, Sylvia. Let's think about this. We've been after Nick to get a part-time job, and if he's getting paid—you are getting paid, right, son?"

"Already put part of the money from the grave robbing story into my savings account."

"What could you make on a story like this? Ballpark figure?"

"Hard to say, Dad. Like I mentioned, it's all based on readership. Might not get paid anything if it turns out to be a hoax."

"But this *Cool Ghoul* thing, you think it's legit?"

"Frank, don't do this."

"Do what?"

"Encourage him. Nick's already said he's here to support Wendy's routine, so drop it."

"Tell me more about the website." Dad passed me the basket of rolls. "How does the owner make money — off ads?"

"He makes some money off ads, but Calvin said the real source of the site's income comes from the virtual gaming community. They share visitor data with role-playing companies and get a kickback. Plus, they have a couple mobile apps that are popular."

Dad, passing the butter to Mom: "I think we should let Nick go, if he wants to."

"Frank!"

"You serious, Dad?"

"Why not? You already said your heart isn't really into watching your sister's performance. Think your company will foot the bill for the airfare?"

"I ... ah ..."

"Call your editor and find out. Then we'll see how hot they are about this story."

Wendy complained, "I knew you'd find a way to make this all about you, Nick."

"It's Dad who's pushing me to do this. I'd be happy riding the Tower of Terror another day."

"Yes, Frank, why are you so anxious to let Nick do something like this?"

"Two words: Aunt Vivian."

"You can't be serious."

"Who's Aunt Vivian?" I asked.

"Dad's scatterbrained aunt," Wendy said. "The one who still thinks you're a girl."

"I thought that was Aunt Effie."

"No, Effie is *my* aunt," Mom said to me.

"Aunt Vivian makes the best sugar cakes," Dad said. "And every Christmas when she sends us her card, she reminds me that I haven't seen her since Mom died. Family is everything, son. May not seem that way now, but it will when you get older."

"What do you say, son? Want to spend a couple of days with your great-aunt?"

"I think you're doing this because you're jealous," Wendy said to me.

"Of what, cheerleading? It's not even recognized as a sport, Wendy."

"Should be," Mom said.

"We could pick you up on our drive home," Dad was saying. "It'd be a little out of our way, but not too much. This *Cool Ghoul* story could be great on your résumé, assuming you don't really uncover a vampire."

"Funny one, Dad."

"Oh, I don't know, Frank. Our little boy, flying on a plane all by himself?" Mom reached her hand across the table and squeezed mine. "Promise me you'll be careful."

"I promise."

"And that you'll phone as you board the plane. And when you land. And when your aunt gets you."

"Yes, Mom. I promise."

"I'm still not comfortable with this," Mom said to Dad. "What if something happens?"

"Come on, Sylvia. How much trouble can he get into?"

"With Nick anything is possible."

CHAPTER TWO
RANDOLPH MANOR

Do like your mom said and call as soon as you land. This is your one shot at proving you can be responsible. Don't blow it."

"Sure, Dad. Thanks for the vote of confidence."

We stood at the end of the security line inside Orlando's International Airport, chitchatting in that awkward way fathers and sons do when neither is sure how to say good-bye. Dad had taken a huge risk letting me fly to Asheville alone, and I knew it. It was one of those "growing up" moments that left Mom worried and Wendy pouting.

"Here's Aunt Vivian's number and address." Dad passed me his business card with her information written on the back.

"Doubt you'll need it. When I asked her to pick you up at the airport, she sounded excited. Went on and on about how she was finally going to get to meet her Nicky."

"You reminded her I'm a guy, right?"

"She remembered. Asked how your arm was healing."

"But I broke it when I was *three*."

"The older you get the harder it is to keep track of things, like time and names. One day you'll understand."

The security line moved forward. It was nearly my turn to place my backpack on the belt. Dad pressed a twenty into my hand.

"We'll start driving up first thing Friday morning. That'll give you a couple of days with your great-aunt and, hopefully, plenty of time to write your article." Dad gave me an awkward hug. "Be careful, Nick. I'd be lost without you, buddy."

"Love you too, Dad."

An hour later I phoned Mom from my departure gate to let her know we were boarding. Then I called again just before the air steward told us to power off all electronic devices. Dad was right: flying to North Carolina on my own was a big deal. Especially since the owner of the *Cool Ghoul Gazette* had paid for my ticket. I knew it must have cost him a lot to buy a ticket on short notice, but Calvin said not to worry, that the owner had used frequent flyer miles. "And besides, he needs the tax write-off for business. The guy's loaded."

A little after ten o'clock our plane touched down in Asheville. Slinging my backpack over my shoulder, I walked outside into the cool Smoky Mountain air and found a blue Chrysler minivan with a dented back fender and a taxi sign on the roof parked near the curb. A pear-shaped woman with white beehive hair struggled to exit the front passenger seat. She wore a loose-fitting blue overcoat, beneath which hung the hem of a bold plaid skirt and white arch-support sneakers. An emerald brooch pinned to the coat's lapel shimmered in the curbside lighting. Sagging off one shoulder was a furry scarf that looked like some flattened roadside fatality.

"Nicky!"

Aunt Vivian?

Layers of mauve eye shadow coated her lids. Scarlet lipstick painted her large lips. She kissed my cheek and hugged me hard. A noxious cloud of perfume engulfed me.

Stepping back, she said, "My, my. Look at you, all grown up. Why, you look just like my sister when she was your age." *Terrific. She still thinks I'm a girl.* Ruffling my hair, she asked, "How old are you now? Sixteen?"

"Fourteen," I answered, pitching my voice as low as possible.

"Your father has told me all about you. Said you are an investigative journalist with an online media company. Sounds important."

"Not really."

"Why, I bet you're the best reporter they have. Come on, let's get started." She took my hand and pulled me along. "I can't wait."

You can't wait? Her grip was firm and warm and for the first time since leaving Dad in Orlando, I relaxed. Dad had told me some about his aunt, but not much. I hadn't seen her since I was three years old. Dad called her a classic southern lady who "will talk your ears off and love on you so hard you'll come home with raw cheeks from where she kissed you so much."

I rolled the door open and crawled into the middle seat.

Aunt Vivian, still chatting about how much I resembled Grandmother Caden — "God rest her soul, I miss her every day" — hoisted herself into the front passenger seat and said to the driver, "Hold on a moment. Here I am carrying on and I haven't even asked you if you needed to use the restroom. We can wait."

I told her I was fine. But just to be safe I asked, "How long is the drive to your house?"

"Oh, that's right. I plumb forgot to tell your father. Knew there was something nagging at me, but I couldn't remember what it was. I was just so excited about having company. That happens when you get old; you forget things. Lately I've started writing stuff down for that very reason. But sometimes there isn't a pen or paper handy and by the time I've found something to write with, whatever I was trying to remember has gone right out of my head." She frowned at me. "Oh dear. Now I've forgotten what you asked me."

"About how long before we get to your house?"

"Pumpkin, there's something you need to know about your Aunt Vivian — which, by the way, is what your father calls me and what I want you to call me. Aunt Vivian, or Aunt Viv.

If you call me your great-aunt, I'll box your ears. 'Great' or 'grand' anything makes me sound old. And I guess I am to some, but when I look in the mirror I still see the same little girl I remember from that farm in South Carolina. Did your grandmother ever tell you about the time the two of us borrowed your great-grandfather's pickup and drove from Sumter to Charleston for the day?"

"I don't remember Grandma Caden ever mentioning a farm."

"That'd be just like her, acting too big for her britches and forgetting where she came from. Like there's something wrong with priming tobacco and getting your hands dirty. Remind me later, I want to show you a picture of your grandmother standing in Battery Park."

"Your house, how long a drive is it?"

"See? Lost track again. Well, child, until they can get my meds regulated, my doctor doesn't want me staying by myself, so I'm living in a retirement center."

"So ... I don't have a place to stay?"

"Oh yes, darlin'. I made a reservation for you at a lovely little bed-and-breakfast. Our wellness director helped me find it online. He's such a nice man. If he wasn't married I would invite him to sit with me on movie night."

I told her thanks and settled into my seat, resting my head against the window. The last thing I remembered hearing was the click-click of the turn signal as we left the airport.

The same clicking sound awoke me. I sat up just as the van turned off a two-lane highway and onto a gravel road. The van's headlights washed over a covered bridge and seconds later loose timbers rumbled beneath the wheels. We pulled into a small parking pad and stopped. In the glare of headlights, a mossy, gray-stone home sat on a small bluff. Low-wattage lighting from the first floor illuminated a pair of drawn shades, and the chimney burped smoke.

I stared at the drab house and suddenly felt ill. "This ... is where I'm staying?"

"Looked different on the website," Aunt Vivian said under her breath.

She hopped out (well, to be honest, she slid out. I couldn't imagine she'd hopped in years) and opened my door. I remained in the van.

"I don't understand. Trip Advisor gave it five stars."

Seriously? Five stars for this dump?

"You go check and make sure someone is still up," said Aunt Vivian. "I'll wait here."

I clutched the strap of my backpack and slowly made my way up a short flight of cracked cement steps. Standing on the front porch, I peeked under the window shade and spied a white-haired man sleeping in a leather chair, mouth open wide, eyeglasses in his lap. A lone tallow candle on a nightstand illuminated his bearded face. I rapped my knuckles on the window. With a jerk he opened his eyes, lifted a hand, and pointed at the door.

Hurrying back to the taxi van, I motioned for Aunt Vivian to roll down her window.

"You sure this isn't a joke?" I asked. "Like maybe something Dad put you up to?"

"Don't you worry, I'm sure everything will be fine. I'll pick you up in the morning and we'll get breakfast."

Yeah, right. Unless you forget.

The van pulled away and I trudged back up the steps, turned the brass knob, and peeked around the door.

"Lock it behind you," the man called to me. "Had a bit of trouble lately with vagrants."

I pushed the door shut and slid the dead bolt into place. To my right was a small dining room, its floor worn, scarred, and uneven. On one wall was a serving counter made of dark wood. Next to the bar was a rack of dusty wine bottles. A chandelier with two bulbs burned out hung over a dining room table. No place settings or any signs of other guests.

"I, ah, have a reservation."

The man lifted his chin to study me. He wore a tan and brown plaid flannel shirt, dark pants, and brown work boots, unlaced. Gray wool socks peeked out from the tongue. He wiped his mouth with the back of his hand and sat up in the chair.

"You must be the new vampire slayer, I reckon. Heard there's one on the way."

"Vampire slayer? No, sir. I'm a reporter for ..." The idea of announcing that I worked for an online publication called the *Cool Ghoul Gazette* seemed silly. "I'm, ah, here, sort of, to investigate a possible murder?"

He hooked the horns of the wire-rim glasses around his large, pink ears. His nose had the broken-vein look of the homeless man who hangs around across the street from our school begging money. Small, dark eyes peered at me from behind the thick lenses.

Stroking his wiry beard, he announced, "Murder, my foot. Suppose some might call it that. More like a mercy killing if you ask me. Sit, boy, you're making me nervous."

I dropped my backpack on the floor and entered the small study, taking a seat across from him. Logs in the fireplace smoldered, their embers glowing orange.

He jabbed them with a poker and said, "Name's Dr. Barlow. Professional pathologist and an expert in vampires. I'm the caretaker of the old Randolph Manor. And you are?"

"Nick Caden. My great-aunt, she made a reservation for me at a B&B, but ..." I glanced around the dirty room. "I'm not sure this was the place she had in mind."

"This is just the guesthouse. Used to be a B&B. Didn't pan out. You'll be staying up the mountain in the manor. Now then, you said you're looking into a murder. Odd. Poor fellow who's dead had a similar tale. Showed up in the middle of the night some months back, same as you. Kept carrying on about bodies rising from graves. Spoke of vampires and such. I warned him to take his foolishness elsewhere. Told him nothing good would come of digging up graves and poking around in old crypts. But he couldn't let it go, and now look at him."

"Speaking of that, what are the chances of me seeing the victim? I mean, who would I speak to about that?"

"County coroner, I suspect. I can't speak as to what's become of the body. I was in Waynesville at the Frankenmuth Festival when I heard. So you have a reservation, do you? Well, sir, you won't find better accommodations than the Randolph Manor, no, sir. I'll take you up there straightaway. But first there are some things you need to know about hunting vampires."

"Hunting vampires?"

"You need any special tools, or did you bring your own?"

"I told you, I'm here investigating a murder." To prove it, I pulled out my investigation notebook. I bring it with me everywhere and am constantly scribbling down notes, facts, and figures. Pulling out a pen, I said, "What can you tell me about the victim? Let's start with his name."

"Barnabas Forester. He owns the manor and guesthouse. Or did. Now that he's dead, not sure what's to become of the estate. So I take it you don't have tools. Not a problem. I'm certain we can find some for you."

"Tools for what?"

"Killing vampires."

"First off, there's no such thing as vampires. And second, did my editor put you up to this?"

"Yes, sir. A lot like Forester, you are. Stubborn and brash. I warned him about digging into the town's dark secrets, I did."

Barlow pushed himself from the chair and ambled toward the foyer. "Wait here. I'll see what I can find in the barn."

The fireplace and logs stacked on the hearth gave the room a warm, rustic feel. I wandered over to the bookshelves and browsed the titles on the spines. All seemed to deal with vampires, werewolves, witches, and mummies. A plaque nailed to the wall identified Dr. Ambrose Barlow as a certified member of the Professional Vampirologist Association. Moments later he returned carrying an old leather medical bag.

I closed a biography of wizards and their recipes for magic potions and said, "Do you really believe there are such things as vampires?"

"Don't much matter what I think. Question is, do you?" He tossed a couple more logs on the fire. "You know, most folks think Lord Byron and Bram Stoker were the first to uncover the curse of the vampire, but others say the origins go back nearly two thousand years, to the time of Christ."

"Oh?"

"Maybe you've heard this before: 'Very truly I tell you, unless you eat the flesh of the Son of Man and drink his blood, you have no life in you.' You remember how he was killed, don't you? Come on, his symbol is everywhere."

"On a cross?" I said hesitantly.

"Not just a cross but a wooden stake," he cried. He stoked the fire and, still kneeling, pivoted to face me. The flame's orange glow gave his face a crazed, demonic appearance.

"I'm not a biblical scholar, but I don't think Jesus really meant we're supposed to drink blood."

"Well, of course not," he said, turning back to the fire. "Anyway, you asked if I believed in vampires. I do. And you will, too, before you leave Transylvania. Now then, grab your backpack and take this medical bag. I need to get you up to the manor."

"So I'm really not going to stay here?"

"First rule of vampire slaying is to begin your hunt where the monster lives. We'd better hurry. Moon will be up soon."

CHAPTER THREE
DARK SHADOWS

Barlow retrieved a long black frock from a coatrack and I followed him out, waiting by the horse-drawn carriage while he pulled the door closed behind him. With a lot of grunting, the innkeeper pulled himself onto the driver's seat and lit the coachman's lantern.

"Well? You coming?"

I remained on the stoop, unsure if I should get in the carriage. The business in Deadwood and the Old West ghost town had forced me to examine certain aspects of the supernatural world, and what I found left me disturbed. Not because I believed in black magic and sorcery—I did not. But many of my friends did.

During my brief time at the *Cool Ghoul*, I'd learned that for every act of spiritual worship, there appeared to be a corresponding ceremony for the occult. It was as if those who practiced witchcraft and participated in séances believed they were tapping into demonic power. But could they really? Was it actually possible for people to give their souls away in exchange for paranormal power? And if so, had Forester?

I climbed into the carriage. Barlow cracked his whip and away we went up a rutted trail. Once we were in the forest, spindly limbs whacked the sides of the carriage and a wispy mist closed in around us. The road leading up the mountain seemed more like a trail than a real road. I'd barely settled into my seat when we crossed a stone bridge and rolled past a cascading waterfall that hissed and spit and left my cheeks and hair damp. In the thickening mist the coach's lantern seemed small and weak.

There comes a point in any journey when you wonder if you've made a mistake, headed off in the wrong direction. For me that moment came as soon as Barlow began rambling about vampires and curses. Right then I should have called Dad and told him to find me a hotel room in Asheville. But I didn't want him to know that Aunt Vivian was living in a nursing home. She'd seemed embarrassed when she'd told me where she was staying. The least I could do was stick it out for one evening.

Outside my window the pale orb of a full moon peeked through the tops of pines and shone down on the fog. Far away there began a low, baritone baying, like the howl of a wolf. I peeked out at the whirling carriage wheels and felt my chest shudder at the sight of large claw prints etched into inky black mud.

Some months earlier I'd read an article about how the federal government wanted to reintroduce red wolves to the Great Smoky Mountains. At the time I thought how awesome it would be to see a park ranger carrying a furry pup to its new den and stapling a GPS tracker to its ear. What I had *not* pictured was a large snarling beast charging through the forest to devour me.

The howling started again, this time coming directly ahead of us. With my heart thumping against the walls of my chest, I glanced at the medical bag and wondered what sort of tools Barlow had included. *Even a pocketknife is better than nothing.* Before I could look, a phantom figure shot past the carriage. Up top I heard Barlow cracking his whip and yelling to the poor horses to hurry. Then...

Wham!

The carriage shuddered.

Whack!

Again something slammed into the carriage. Growing more worried by the second, I looked down and saw a beastly creature sprinting alongside the carriage, its ears erect and black snout glistening. Huge paws ripped up chunks of dirt as it ran. The thing that drew my attention, though, were the fangs and the way they shimmered with saliva. I had no experience with wolves, only knew them from watching the Nature Channel, but even in a full run I knew this was no ordinary wolf. It was much too large.

As quickly as we'd entered the fog, the carriage exploded from the mist and went rocketing across a grassy meadow. I took a final look back at the woods and saw the beast pacing along the tree line, eyes glowing yellow in the fading light of the lantern. No sooner had I settled back in my seat than the moon shone down upon a mansion perched along the crest of the ragged ridge. Darkened windows looked out upon a court-yard overgrown with weeds. Vines crept up gray walls. No sign of cars or movement of any kind.

Barlow guided the carriage over a stone bridge guarded by gargoyles and under a stone archway. The clomping of the horses' hooves on the cobblestone drive echoed off stone walls. The carriage stopped and Barlow dismounted. I didn't move, not a muscle. I kept thinking that any minute flood-lights would come on and people would burst from behind the thorny hedge and shout, "SURPRISE!"

My door opened and I gazed up at the mansion. A cool night breeze skipped dry leaves across slate steps. Scraggly rose-bushes with shriveled petals bracketed the front landing. Bare wires from a busted porch light dangled over the wooden door.

"This is a joke, right?"

"Don't forget your tools," Barlow said, grabbing the medi-cal bag from my lap. "Your life depends on it."

"Did my dad put you up to this?"

Barlow took my elbow and pulled me from the carriage. Clutching the straps of my backpack, I studied his face, looking for any sign of humor.

"You can't possibly expect me to stay here. Where are the botanical gardens and the fountains and the rocking chairs for the guests? Where's the pool? Where are all the, you know ... people?"

"Wait right here. I'll see if your room is ready."

He ambled up the steps and went inside the mansion, leaving me alone by the carriage. Clouds moved across the moon. The breeze worked its way across the courtyard and whipped my bangs. Far away, the howling began again. I pulled out my phone but the service indicator showed one bar, then none, one then none. A crow flew overhead, squawking, as though mocking me. Hooking the strap of my backpack through one arm I picked up the medical bag and started walking until I reached the front door.

"Hey, is there a light switch somewhere I can turn on?"

The moon's slanting gray light cast my shadow across a hardwood floor. I paused in the doorway and waited for my eyes to adjust.

"Yo, Dr. Barlow, did you get lost?"

After several seconds I could make out portraits hanging on paneled walls. Doorways opened off the hallway. A wide carpet runner led from the front door toward the rear of the house. A suffocating stillness settled over the house. Gradually my night vision improved. To my right was something like a front parlor with a couch and chairs. To my left two open doors lead to a study. The wind fell away and it occurred to me the howling had ceased. Then standing in the doorway of the darkened mansion I understood why.

Click, click, click

Hard claws tap-tap-tapped on the porch landing's stone steps. My silhouette in the moon's shadow expanded to include the bulk of a large creature standing behind me. Warm breaths misted my palm. A low growl chilled me. Without moving my head, not an inch, I looked out of the corner of my eyes and saw the animal's lips pulled back. Fangs glowed white in moonlight. I smelled the stench of decay in its fur. Yellow eyes studied me, then narrowed as if the animal was preparing to pounce.

"Moses, heel!"

I jumped at the sound of the Barlow's voice. A halo of candlelight appeared at the top of the staircase.

"Heel, I say!"

Barlow descended the staircase. The animal took a step away from me and settled onto its haunches.

"My apologies if Moses frightened you. I should have mentioned we have a guard dog."

My eyes remained on the creature. Each one of its enormous claws was the thickness of my thumb.

Stepping past me, Barlow pushed the door shut. "All set to go, this way."

The wolf dog followed Barlow up the staircase. I hung back, remaining at the edge of the light's halo. I wanted to keep some distance between the animal and me in case it wheeled around and attacked. We reached the second floor and turned right. Moonlight leaked through the window at the far end of the hallway. Floorboards creaked under our weight. *Click, click, click* went the wolf dog's claws tap-tapping down the hallway.

We stopped at the end of the hall and entered a front bedroom overlooking the drive. The room actually looked pretty nice. Four-poster bed, nightstand, a porcelain washbasin. Frosted windowpanes were covered with bars. Barlow lit a candle on the dresser and said to me, "I trust you will enjoy your stay at Randolph Manor. Remember what I told you: Stay away from cemeteries, morgues, and crypts. Do that and you might make it out of Transylvania alive."

"Wait! Let me go back with you. I'll sleep on the floor by the fireplace, or in a chair. Anyplace but here."

"You want to hunt vampires, don't you?"

"No!"

Too late. The door clicked shut. Barlow locked it from the other side.

His footsteps had barely faded before I hurried over and pushed a chair and storage trunk against the door. I looked at my phone and silently pleaded with my service provider to blow a signal my direction. No luck. Next I looked inside the medical bag and found a wooden stake, woodworking mallet, and garlic cloves in a plastic baggie. Someone was obviously playing a joke on me, probably Dad. I kicked off my sneakers and rummaged through my backpack for my phone charger.

I was about to blow out the candle when I saw the small brown leather-bound book on the nightstand. Across the front in faded gold lettering were the words, *Vampire Mythology: The Curse of Darkness*. I built a nest of pillows against the headboard and picked up the book. A handwritten note fluttered onto my chest.

> If you are reading this note, it means you have arrived at the Randolph Manor. This is a mistake but not an accident. You were brought here for a purpose ... one that I will explain in a moment.

> No doubt the manor is dark and empty and you are alone, except for that hideous beast that prowls the halls. Do not try to leave by the front door; it is locked. There is no way out now, except one. I pray you find it before the monster rises to feed.

I felt the hairs on my neck prickling.

> When I first arrived, I, too, believed this business of vampires roaming the countryside was a joke: some elaborate charade to lure tourists to Transylvania. But soon I learned the rumors are true and the curse, deadly.

> Fear the darkness, for it is in the black hearts of men that evil lurks. The monster you seek feeds on the innocent and pure of heart. Should this

vile curse spread to our young—as I fear it has already—their unnatural cravings and perverted lusts will destroy us.

Of course if you are reading this note, then you know I am dead. I suppose that alone should motivate you to take my warning seriously. I encourage you to escape now while you still can, for if you do not, you too may find yourself forever bound by the curse of darkness.

The note was signed *Barnabas Forester*.

I tucked the scrap of paper back into the vampire book and, stretching out on the bed, thought of how ironic it was that I'd found another note from the grave. Just like Deadwood Canyon. I blew out the candle and sank onto the bed, tightly clutching the mallet and wooden stake in case, you know ... *this isn't Dad's idea of a joke.*

CHAPTER FOUR
MORTIFIED AT THE MORGUE

I woke up Thursday morning at 7:11. I'd made it through the night without getting bitten by a vampire. I flipped open Forester's leather journal and started reading where I'd left off the night before.

> The word "vampire" is a relatively new term. Tales of blood-drinking supernatural demons and ghosts were rampant in Mesopotamia, ancient Greece, and India long before Jesus Christ. The Akhkharu were rumored to be blood-sucking demons. In ancient Chinese culture there are stories of corpses hopping from one victim to another.

Even ancient Egyptian lore had a story where the goddess Sakhmet lusted after the blood of humans.

I tucked the journal into my back pants pocket, pushed aside the chair and dresser, and tried the door. The knob turned easily. I peeked into the hallway, ready to spring back at the sight of the wolf dog, but found the corridor empty. After a quick rinse in a claw-foot bathtub, I changed into my last pair of clean jeans and pulled on a blue long-sleeve tee.

The manor didn't seem nearly as scary by day, just old and unkempt. I crept down the long staircase and listened for the click-click of claws approaching. In the entrance hall, dusty drapes woven from heavy fabric covered floor-to-ceiling windows. Spiderwebs glistened between banister spindles. I checked the front door and found it locked, just as Forester's note said.

I wandered through the main part of the house, checking each room, testing every latch and lock and window. In the banquet hall I found china settings, wineglasses, and silverware placed around a long dinner table. Tapestries covered the walls. A pipe organ dominated the music studio; in the billiard room, I saw an oil painting of dogs playing poker. Chess pieces sat on a dirty game board. The mansion seemed to have everything but an exit. Only one room remained unexplored, the room by the front door.

Dark-paneled doors swung open and I snapped pictures with my phone's camera. Bookcases on two walls, green drapes over the windows. Spiderwebs knitted over an empty fireplace. On an ornately carved desk a silver chandelier sat with hardened dollops of wax. The room had the smell of musty books and soot and another odor, like that of a stinky, wet dog. Gray hair, like dog hair, covered the crimson rug. There was considerable wear on the hardwood floor along one corner of the rug, so I dropped to one knee and lifted it.

A metal latch sat in a divot carved into polished wood planking. It had been designed to rest flush on the floor, leaving no hint of the latch beneath the rug. I smiled at the genius of it. Who would have thought to look for a cellar door in the study?

With a twist of the lever, a catch released and a section of the floor raised a few inches. I pulled the trapdoor the rest of the way up and, using my phone's light application, illuminated a staircase. Rounded steps spiraled downward between crumbling brick walls. Water seeped through chipped masonry. Taking a deep breath, I started down.

The staircase made one full revolution before leveling off. I swept my light across blackened stone tiles and walked down the cramped hallway until I reached a large room with a low ceiling. Overhead, cobwebs clung to heavy floor joists. A dressing mirror stood in a corner. On the floor, a squatting candle sat beside a dusty black coffin.

The wolf dog lay between the coffin and me with ears erect and eyes watching. It lifted its head and emitted a low growl. The clinking of chain links scraping on hard stone revealed a short chain and U-bolt cemented into the stone flooring. The beast was on a short leash. *Thank God!* Switching apps, I snapped pictures of the coffin and wolf dog. At the flash, the wolf dog sprang onto all fours and moved not toward me, as I'd feared, but closer to the coffin.

"Easy, boy, you can keep whatever's in that coffin. I'm just trying to get out of here without getting bit by you ... or anything else."

I reactivated the flashlight app and aimed it at a second opening across the room. Flattening myself against the wall, I crept sideways and slunk away from the animal. At the edge of the open doorway, I snapped one final picture of the wolf dog standing next to the coffin, then ducked into the tunnel and hurried off.

Stone flooring gave way to hard-packed dirt. Once I thought I heard the click-click-clicking again, but when I swept the light behind me, all I saw were rats. The tunnel sloped downward and ended in a crude drainage system. Rusty pipes jutted out of earthen walls and dripped into a shallow trench.

The trench became an underground spring. I don't know how long I walked. As I walked I thought of something we'd gone over in my social studies class. Apparently during the Civil War, Union sympathizers in the Appalachian Mountains helped slaves escape to the North. I wondered if I was walking an ancient underground trail or merely rushing toward a dead end that would force me to backtrack. After a long twisting section, I came to a shallow trench filled with bones and skulls.

Maybe human—it was hard to tell, some were so tiny. The deer heads were the easiest to identify.

A short ways past the skulls, I came to an opening partially covered with vines and bushes. I crawled out and emerged on a ledge overlooking the cedar-shingled roof of the guesthouse.

I found Aunt Vivian knitting in the driver's seat of a pearl-colored Cadillac.

"Did you sleep well, dear?" A knitting bag sat beside her. Wearing a purple blouse, cream-colored slacks, and white walking shoes, she looked elegant.

I reached over and turned the keys in the ignition. "Let's go."

"Oh, it couldn't have been that bad."

"I have to know, is Dad the one who told you to book me a room in that place?" I buckled my seat belt. "It's okay if he did."

"No, darlin', I promise. Your dad had nothing to do with it. Why? Did something happen?"

"Rather not talk about it." I took a final look at the guesthouse and saw Barlow watching me from the upstairs window. To Aunt Vivian, I said, "Can you drop me off at the medical examiner's office? There's someone there dying to meet me."

Transylvania did not have a medical examiner. What they did have was a coroner working out of a single-story, brick-and-glass office building on the corner of Morrison and Main.

Aunt Vivian parked in a handicap spot and opened her car door as if to come inside with me.

"I can do this myself."

She patted me on the shoulder and said, "I'm sure you can, hon."

"Really, Aunt Vivian. I'd *rather* go it alone."

"Sugar, do you have any idea what it's like to be my age?"

I confessed I did not.

"At my age you can't see or hear. Your *friends* can't see or hear. You spend all day in a room full of deaf and blind and comatose retirees who sit around a TV that no one can work except Mr. Spencer — who used to own a television repair shop — and who complains loudly to anyone who *can* hear that the last really good show on television was *Hee Haw.* Then when Mr. Spencer *does* decide to switch channels to something really good, like the *Andy Griffith Show,* inevitably somebody yells: 'Hey, why'd you change the channel?' So we go back to watching overweight women with peach fuzz on their upper lip complain about how they can't get a date. Except they don't say *date,* if you know what I mean."

I did.

"Meanwhile, I wander back to my room and look in the mirror and see Lady Bird Johnson looking back at me. Do you know how depressing that is?"

"Who's Lady Bird Johnson?"

"See? This is what I'm talking about. Life is passing me

by. And don't get me started on the horny codgers prowling around in that place."

"Okay, I won't."

Aunt Vivian got out and locked the car, then said to me, "Walk me inside."

I hurried around and took her arm.

"Most of the men on my hall smell like they haven't bathed since the Nixon administration. They walk around with their pants pulled up to their armpits, which makes them look like paratroopers about to invade France. And that's really sad because I know good and well some of them *did* fight in World War II but their families don't seem to care. Boys your age can't even pull up their pants."

I wasn't about to get into a style discussion with Aunt Vivian over the social significance of "sagging." I held the door open for Aunt Vivian and she shuffled into the lobby.

"I wake up at four and can't go back to sleep because when I look in the mirror I see this wrinkled, white-haired person and so I sit in the kitchen reading my Bible until the morning news shows come on. Sometimes I'll pray for your father. He was such a sweet boy growing up. I wonder why he never calls or writes."

"He's busy. We all are. I hear him tell Mom all the time how busy they are."

"But not too busy to go to Florida on a vacation?"

"We did that for my sister."

"Just saying, hon, we make time for the things that matter." She stopped and patted me on the cheek. "But don't you worry.

I'm not going to make your father feel guilty for not visiting, I promise. Now then, I'll be in one of those chairs over there, knitting. You won't even know I'm here, I promise."

While Aunt Vivian deployed needles and yarn, I told a dour-faced woman behind the sliding glass window that I was there to view Forester's body. She asked me how I was related to the deceased and I explained my position with the *Cool Ghoul Gazette*. She placed a call and I waited.

In a few minutes a door opened and a round little man with reading glasses perched atop his bald head entered through a side door. He had a chubby, double-chinned face and looked to be anywhere between thirty and forty. I strolled over and he introduced himself as Dr. Arthur Edwards. Dad says you can tell a lot about a man by the way he shakes your hand. The doctor's grip was limp and sweaty. He wore a brown suit, scuffed black dress shoes, and a look of irritation.

"I am afraid I cannot allow you to view the body. Authorized personnel only. Unless you are an immediate member of the family—are you?"

"No, sir, but I would only be a few minutes."

"No media, sorry."

Aunt Vivian looked up from her knitting. "My nephew traveled a long way. Flew all the way up from Florida."

"Yes, ma'am, I understand," Dr. Edwards said, "but there are rules."

"Rules my foot. I bet if he was whatshisname, that handsome man on *Good Morning News*, you'd bend the rules."

Dr. Edwards cut his eyes toward me. I shrugged to let him know *I* didn't know what guy she was talking about either.

"Oh, don't look at me that way, you know who I'm talking about. Dimpled chin, boyish face? Has really nice teeth and a funny name I can't pronounce?"

"Even if your nephew was this individual," Edwards said to Aunt Vivian, "I still could not allow him to see the body."

She sighed, put down her knitting, and ambled over. Reaching into her purse, she pulled out a church-offering envelope and slipped five twenty-dollar bills inside.

One hundred dollars?

"I can only imagine how expensive it must be to run for the office of county coroner," she said to Edwards. "My late husband was on our local school board back in Asheville. He loved kids but hated politics." She pressed the envelope into the doctor's sweaty palm. "This is for your reelection campaign. It's not much but maybe this will help buy a few yard signs."

Edwards pocketed the envelope without smiling. "I will speak with my assistant."

"Mind if I ask you a couple of questions?"

Reaching for the door handle, he stopped and turned back toward me. "Yes, I do mind."

"I'll make it quick. The victim, I understand he's been identified as Barnabas Forester."

"I cannot confirm that. You'll need to speak to Lieutenant McAlhany regarding the particulars of the deceased."

"Did you know the victim?"

Edwards glanced at his watch and made a nervous twitching noise with his teeth that sounded like a rabbit nibbling a carrot.

"Not really. I know his wife. She and I helped chair a breast cancer awareness event last fall. Lucy has a gallery here in town. From the way she talked, her husband was something of a recluse."

"So you and the victim's wife, you are friends?"

"Lucy?" For a split second his look of irritation faded. "Of course." The scowl returned. "Look, are you writing a story or investigating this man's death?"

"Both. I'm part of a group that analyzes television shows — crime shows in particular." I explained how we cataloged the shows and fed the information into our database. "With that information I can run a query of all shows that match certain variables. Like in this case, now that I know he was married, we have a dead husband as the victim, a spooky mansion, a strange-acting innkeeper, those sorts of things. Once I have all the variables, I review any episodes that match those elements."

Edwards looked over at Aunt Vivian and back at me. "I cannot imagine that works."

"It does, actually."

"Look, I have to go," he said dryly. "I have *real* work to do."

When the doctor was gone I said to Aunt Vivian, "You shouldn't have paid him. I could have talked him into letting me see the body on my own."

"It's just money, dear. I can't take it with me, and where I'm going they pave the streets with gold."

"But it's bribery."

"Be wise as serpents and harmless as doves."

"What does *that* mean?"

"Remind me later and I'll explain it to you."

Aunt Vivian had barely picked up her needles when a girl appeared in the doorway. She wore a white long-sleeved turtleneck under blue scrubs and lime green Crocs and introduced herself as the doctor's assistant. Aunt Vivian and I followed her into a brightly lit hallway, through two sets of double doors, and down a stairwell. The assistant badged in and flipped a switch, activating a bank of overhead fluorescent lights.

Three empty stainless steel gurneys stood parked along one wall. To the left of the door a gooseneck lamp sat on the corner of a desk covered with manila folders. Beside the desk, medical trays sat on a polished metal counter. Though it wasn't my first trip to a morgue, I still felt anxious. Not scared, just curious about the condition of the body.

"This won't take long," I said, leaving Aunt Vivian by the door.

The assistant crossed the room and went to a bank of vaults. There were six polished steel doors in all, three columns wide, two rows high. No mistaking we were in a morgue — the chill and smell of cleaning solvents gave it away.

"Dr. Edwards tells me you watch TV and solve crimes?"

The assistant had long, straight auburn-brown hair, a pout, and freckles dusting her cheeks, nose, and forehead.

"In my spare time, yes. In fact, a couple months ago I solved a murder in Deadwood Canyon. That's an Old West reenactment ghost town in Colorado. I discovered a body in the hayloft, but when the marshal went to look, it was gone. No one believed me, not even my family. They all thought it was part of the disappearing-cowboy-ghost act, but I eventually found the killer. I'm Nick Caden, by the way. And you are ..."

"Busy."

She opened the metal door. The drawer rolled easily on bearings, clicking into the track-stop. I stepped closer and studied the lumpy shape beneath the sheet.

"Can I see?" Aunt Vivian asked.

We turned and looked at her.

"It's not every day someone my age gets the chance to help solve a murder."

"The thing is, Mrs. ...."

"Vivian is fine, dear. 'Mrs.' anything makes me sound old. And I didn't catch your name, hon."

"Meg."

I locked eyes with Aunt Vivian and gave her just the slightest smile to let her know I appreciated the subtle way she'd gotten the assistant to tell us her name.

"The thing is, I shouldn't even be showing *him* the body. I'm sure Dr. Edwards explained our policy."

"Child, if you spend all your life following the rules, you'll end up a dull Delilah."

"A dull what?"

"She's talking about that sappy radio host who gives out relationship advice," I said. "Come on, *Meg*, let her have a look."

"It would make the women in my prayer group so jealous," Aunt Vivian added. "Those ladies never do anything fun. Please?"

"Okay, but if I get fired over this, I'm blaming you," Meg said to me.

"Get in line."

We huddled around the body and watched as the sheet folded back to the victim's waist. I admit, I wasn't prepared for the condition of the body and for a few seconds my skin had that clammy feeling I get right before I'm going to vomit.

Aunt Vivian put her hand to her mouth and said, "Dear Lord."

I choked down bile and framed the body on my phone's screen but couldn't make my thumb press the button.

The victim appeared to be in his early forties. Thick, reddish-brown bangs, skin the color of oatmeal. Chest and cheeks deflated from the lack of blood. Eyes milky white slits. On television they'll often close the eyes of the dead. It's a touching scene that hardly ever works in real life. Once dead, eyelids sag like a window shade, stopping about halfway down. The sight can be unsettling to family members viewing the body, so funeral homes will usually glue the eyelids shut, and superglue the lips together.

No one had taken such care with Barnabas Forester. The

sight of Forester laid out on the cold, slab of steel sickened me. I pocketed my phone. Calvin would howl once he found out I'd skipped the chance to snap a shot, but he'd have to get over it. Make light of something as precious as life, and you cheapen yourself.

"Mercy, mercy," Aunt Vivian said softly.

I leaned over and examined the puncture wound in his chest. The weapon had left a jagged crater in his chest, exposing bone and tissue and a pummeled mass of what I assumed was the heart. The entry point was as big around as a half dollar and slightly concaved where hardened flesh curled inward.

I captured it all with my mind's eye.

"Cause of death?" I asked. "Sounds stupid, I know, but I need to verify for the article."

"Just like it looks. Stab wound to the chest."

"Any sign of blunt-force trauma to the head? Like maybe someone knocked him out first, then stabbed him? Evidence of a struggle, maybe?"

"Not that we can tell. Dr. Edwards checked for tissue under the nails. They're clean. But then, we're not set up to do an autopsy here."

"Did he bleed out at the scene?" I saw the surprised look on her face. "What I mean is, if the victim *was* a vampire — not that I believe in that sort of thing — but if he was, then the lack of blood might be important to the story."

"I honestly don't know."

"Who called it in?"

"Again, I do not know."

"How about the murder weapon? Do you know anything about *that*?"

"Are you always this obnoxious?"

"Only on Wednesdays."

"Today is Thursday."

"I'm expanding my range."

"There was a wooden stake in his chest. Dr. Edwards thinks it might be white pine or maybe spruce. But I believe it was put there after death. Forensics will tell us more. The weapon and victim's clothes were sent to the police."

"How about his teeth? Anything odd there?"

"See for yourself."

With the tip of a pencil she carefully lifted Forester's upper lip, exposing two fangs. Both tapered to a needle-sharp tip. They certainly looked real, but I had a hunch they were fake and glued on with denture cement, just like the ones sold in Halloween stores.

"Have you tested the gums for glue residue?"

"Dr. Edwards wondered about that too. When I got buzzed to come up, I thought that was the oral surgeon from Asheville arriving to inspect the body. Then there's this."

Using a gloved hand Meg rolled the victim's head toward us and touched a place on the right side of his neck just below his jaw.

"Bite marks?" I asked.

"I feel light-headed," Aunt Vivian said. "I think I'm going

to wait by the door." She waddled away, leaving the two of us together with the body exposed.

"The puncture marks are pretty recent but occured before the time of death." With her pencil she touched the victim's neck. "See this discoloration? Indicates it was starting to heal."

"Wow. Bite marks and fangs."

The assistant rolled the body back into the drawer and hustled us out of the morgue.

Back in the lobby I said, "Is there anything else you can tell me about the victim?"

"Like?"

"Where he lived, any strange habits he might have had? How he made a living?" She frowned as though wondering if she could trust me. "Come on, I'm not going to get you in trouble, I swear."

"Sure, okay, but if you quote me, I'll ... do something. Not sure what, but it won't be pleasant."

"Nick, honey, I'm going to step into the ladies room, if that's okay."

"Take your time." I waited until Aunt Vivian was gone, then said, "You were saying ..."

"Last winter a few of us snuck up to the Randolph Manor. You know where that is?"

"I do."

"The boy I was with thought it might be fun to poke around. The place is rumored to be haunted, but what old house isn't, right? Anyway, normally I wouldn't be caught dead doing something like that, but he'd been helping me with a report on geothermal electricity. We were studying how the rate of radioactive decay can serve as a predictor of fossil fuel reserves. I don't suppose any of that makes sense to you."

"The earth's heat naturally flows to the surface and the speed of decomposition below the crust can increase the pressure, thus causing gases to press against the magma." I grinned at her. "I watch the Nature Channel sometimes."

"So anyway, according to my study buddy, the Randolph place sits on pockets of magma conduits and hydrothermal circulation. There's supposed to be some old mine shafts under there, but we never had a chance to check it out. As soon as we arrived we began hearing weird noises."

"Like?"

"Someone screaming, footsteps running, things breaking. I got scared and made him take me home. Haven't been back since. If you really want to know about the manor, you should speak with the owner of Dead Lines Books. He's like the town's local historian."

"Last question. Estimated time of death?"

"Sometime between twelve and four a.m."

"So before sunrise."

"Wow, aren't you the sharp one."

"Now look who's being snooty."

Smiling, she replied, "I pick up things quickly."

"Can I get your last name for the story?"

"Just say 'a source within the medical community.'"

"Last question, I promise. Do you get a lunch break?"

"Are you asking me out?"

"Oh yeah, sure. You and me and my aunt. See, the thing is, I don't know anybody in the area and I was thinking you could h—"

"Sure, sure, that's fine. Twelve thirty. I'll meet you out front."

I walked outside and waited by the car, thinking about how upset Calvin was going to be when he learned I didn't have any pictures of the body. I could give him a written description of the victim and play up the bit about fangs and bite marks, but without photos it might not matter. Sorry, buddy, but I'm not a Paparazzi photographer and hope I'll never become one.

When Aunt Vivian reached the car, I said, "If it's okay, I'd like to walk to the bookstore. Need some time to think."

"I'll be at the Red Wolf Gallery. I hardly ever get a chance to shop anymore, and the stores in this little town look so interesting."

"Aunt Vivian, thanks again for what you did back there with the doctor and getting the assistant to tell us her name. Dad was right. You're the greatest great-aunt of all time."

"Bless your heart. Your father said this murder business was important to you. And honestly, this is fun. Beats watching TV all day. Now run along and find that poor man's killer. I cannot wait to tell the girls in my prayer group that I'm part of a criminal investigative unit. They'll be so jealous."

CHAPTER FIVE
DEATH—BY HOOK OR BOOK

I ducked under the vine-shaded canopy of a lattice arbor and followed the pebble footpath through a maze of landscaped ground cover. Beside a goldfish pond, classical music played through plastic speakers made to look like river stones. Customers sat on benches and in Adirondack chairs reading books and drinking coffee. The owner of Dead Lines Books had gone to a lot of trouble to create a relaxed environment, and it appeared to be working.

I paused midway across the short archway bridge and scanned another section of Forester's vampire journal. If I was going to solve the mystery surrounding Forester's death, I needed to learn all I could about the legend of the Dark Curse.

The fear of vampires and the desire for eternal life is as old as humankind itself. Perhaps the most well-known story is the Garden of Eden. Adam and Eve are presented with a choice: enjoy all creation except for the fruit from the tree of good and evil and live forever. "But if you eat its fruit," God says, "you will die."

According to the story, the young couple disobeyed God and he banished them from the garden. Then God ordered angels to stand in front of the tree of life to prevent the pair from living in a state of eternal damnation. Thus began humankind's quest to secure immortality.

In ancient Persia there has been found artwork depicting a man struggling with a monstrous blood-sucker. In Jewish mythology there is the legend of Lilith—a female demon who, according to some early Christian traditions, may have been the serpent in the Garden of Eden. The character of Lilith is believed to have inspired the Sumerian myths about female vampires called "Lillu" or Mesopotamian myths about succubae (female night demons) called "lilin."

Forester had certainly been right about one thing: human-kind's infatuation with vampires and evil began long before Bram Stoker wrote *Dracula*.

I stepped into the bookstore, causing a cowbell to jingle overhead. The shop was long and narrow with brick walls and hardwood floors. Rolling ladders reached to top shelves. The rich aroma of freshly brewed coffee mixed with the pungent smell of new books.

Printing ink is one of those truly underrated smells. Older books still have it, but in new books the smell fades quickly. I learned this last Christmas while working in the shipping department of a local book printer. We have this rule in our family: children spend their own money for gifts. No hitting Mom or Dad up for Christmas shopping money. My parents don't care what I buy them. It can be a ten-dollar gift card to Starbucks, but it has to be something I purchased with money I earned or something I made myself.

Same rule for my sister. I have a drawer full of hand-painted picture frames I'll never use.

From Thanksgiving to Christmas last winter, I worked at the print shop and learned a lot about books—or at least a lot about how books are printed. Every time Mom complains about boys my age not reading anymore, I want to scream, "Give me a break."

And I mean it. I need a break from reading. It's all I do. I read textbooks and tests and term papers. My school forces me to read awful novels because there's this requirement that says every student must read a certain number of books by the end of the grading period. Do you have any idea how hard it is to find an "approved" book that's interesting? No wonder books about boy wizards and teen vampires and children killing each other are so popular. At least the stories are *interesting*.

"May I help you?"

I stopped scanning the back cover of a book called *The Incomplete Idiot's Guide to Natural Cures, Curses, and Potions*.

"You the owner?"

"Yes, Phillip Raintree. Finding everything okay?"

Raintree was a lean man of medium height with curly blond hair tinged with gray. He wore wire-rim glasses with round lenses. He had on a green tartan vest over a white dress shirt, faded jeans, and Birkenstock sandals with gray socks.

"Do you have any books on the history of this area?"

He flashed a toothy, nicotine-stained grin. "Was there a particular era you're interested in? We carry an extensive collection that covers the early years dating all the way back to when the Cherokee inhabited this area. Makes for an interesting read. Is this for a class project?"

Ignoring his question, I asked, "Anything more recent?"

"There's also an excellent set of works that covers from the Revolutionary War to the antebellum era."

"I was thinking more along the lines of the town's beginnings; how it got its name, the history of prominent figures, family secrets, and that sort of thing."

"Wait right here."

I went back to reading the instructions for how to cause a wart to sprout on someone's nose by mixing celery, cumin, and goat cheese. The accompanying pictures looked hideous.

But hey, if I really could learn to grow a wart on my sister's nose
… Raintree returned with a hardback with gold-tipped pages.

"Everything you could ever want to know about Transylvania
is in here. The writing is a bit dry, but the author did a thorough
job of documenting his sources. This book is quite rare. Published
in the early nineteen hundreds. Out of print, of course. Lucky for
you, we have one of the few remaining copies available."

"Does it explain how the town got its name?"

"Of course. But you do not need a book for that. Transylvania is derived from the Latin phrase *trans* meaning 'across'
and *sylva* meaning 'woods.' As you have no doubt noticed, we
are surrounded by woods and rolling hills. Any suggestion that
our town is linked to the region in Romania and the so-called
birthplace of vampires is purely unintentional."

"But not unwelcome."

His smile faded. "Excuse me?"

"This shop, these books." I nodded toward the rack of vampire novels. "Having a bookstore known as Dead Lines in a
place called Transylvania can't be a coincidence."

"Oh, I suppose a few customers *do* drop in hoping to find
books on the supernatural. And I did choose the name for
obvious marketing reasons. But I assure you books of that
nature make up only a small portion of our sales. Romance
novels and historical fiction is where we make our money."

I put the idiot's potions book back on the shelf and gave
him one of my *Cool Ghoul Gazette* business cards.

He studied the card, frowning.

Before he could brush me off, I said, "My editor sent me because he thought the victim was a vampire. What do you think?"

Raintree tucked the card into his vest pocket and glanced away, as if anxious to get back to helping other customers. "I do not speculate on things of which I have no knowledge or interest."

"But you did hear about the body they found, right?"

How could he not? He ran a bookstore dealing in the dead and the occult. If he denied knowing about Forester's death, that could only mean one thing: he was in on it.

"Of course. It's not every day a body is found staked to a putting green."

"What can you tell me about Randolph Manor?"

His eyes widened, making me wonder if my comment had knocked him off stride.

"I ... ah ... know of the place, sure. Some years ago I expressed an interest in purchasing the property. Not that I could ever afford to own it outright. There isn't *that* much money in selling books. But as a lark I formed a nonprofit organization and appointed myself chair and began soliciting funding to establish a conservancy on the land. The town council thought it was a wonderful idea and gave me their blessing. The idea was to turn the property into a wildlife preserve. You may not know this, but the U.S. Fish and Wildlife Service is reintroducing red wolves to this area. They, along with black bear and coyote, have been almost hunted into extinction.

"Once I had secured adequate financial commitments, I approached the two owners with what I believed was a generous offer. The two Randolph brothers made it clear neither had any intention of selling. I dissolved the nonprofit soon thereafter and put all my energies into making this store a success. That's the extent of what I know about Randolph Manor."

"So who owns it now, the same two brothers?" I knew the answer, but I wanted to see if Barlow's story lined up with the Raintree's.

"I should say not. Not long after the Randolph brothers rejected my bid, the younger of the two brothers ran into financial difficulties and petitioned the court to dissolve his grandfather's agreement. The patriarch of the family, Rupert Randolph, had deeded the estate to the two grandsons in such a way that precluded either heir from selling their half of the estate without the other's permission. The younger Randolph grandson argued that he was paying property taxes on an asset that he could not sell nor afford to maintain. The judge ruled in his favor and shortly thereafter the brother sold his half of the mountain to a consortium of investors led by Victor Hamilton. The ink was hardly dry on the agreement before the trucks and tractors rolled in and began knocking down trees and building that revolting golf course resort."

"So your offer was too early."

"And woefully underfunded. Our small nonprofit never would have paid what Hamilton's people did. His group had some serious backers. Shame, too. He created such a mess of the streams that the North Carolina Department of Environment and Natural Resources threatened to shut him down."

"What about the manor and the land around it? Did this fellow Hamilton buy that too?"

"Actually, no. When the elder Randolph brother became ill last summer, he put his half of the mountain up for sale. There was a nasty bidding war between Hamilton's people and a man from up north, Barnabas Forester."

Now my eyebrows shot up. I could almost feel myself leaning in, listening harder.

"Of course by then I had long since lost interest. The whole matter was, as they say, too rich for my blood."

"So Forester bought the manor?"

"Indeed he did. It tickled me to no end to see Hamilton bested at his own game."

"Sounds like Forester had money?"

"It would seem. And now he is dead, which I suppose is the point of all your questions."

"Did you ever meet him?"

"Forester? He came in once asking questions and inquiring about certain books, much as you are doing right now."

"What types of books?"

"Old burial grounds. Historic churches. I remember him behaving strangely."

"Strange in what way?"

"He carried a leather satchel and refused to put it down. Kept it in his hand at all times."

"Do you know if he did much work on the manor after he bought it? Or if anyone else was living with Forester?"

"To my knowledge, no. Rumor has it Forester and his wife purchased the property and moved into the guesthouse. Maybe they planned to fix up the mansion; I can't say for sure. As I mentioned, I only saw him a few times. But unless I'm badly mistaken, no one has lived in the manor since before the elder Randolph passed away."

I could tell he was getting antsy by the way he kept shifting his weight and glancing around the store, so I hurried to get in my last few questions. "And Mrs. Forester? Do you know much about her?"

"Lucy? Yes, of course." He pointed out the front window. "Down that street and to your left you will find her gallery. She is quite famous, you know. Her works are on display in New York and Paris. And all over town, of course. She has her art studio behind her home. For a while she and Forester tried to turn the guesthouse into a bed-and-breakfast. I've never met two people more ill suited to be in the hospitality business."

Feigning surprise I asked, "So the B&B is closed?"

"I think Lucy knew that venture was doomed from the start. That's why she returned to the little house she had been renting in town. As I said, Mr. Forester was somewhat eccentric. I can imagine he might have been difficult to work with."

"You mean 'live with,'" I said, correcting him.

"That too. I was thinking about the couple's strained business relationship."

Nodding toward the clippings next to the register, I said, "Couldn't help but notice that you're something of an authority on vampires. Does the store have a website?"

"Of course. Any business that does not have a presence on the Web will not be in business for long. We also have a smartphone app and are active in social media. Now then, is there anything I can show you in the way of reading material?"

His comment was an obvious dig at my persistent questioning, but if I was going to get to the truth, it couldn't be helped.

"One more question. Did you kill Forester?"

"Don't be absurd—of course not. I was out of town the night it happened. I explained all this to the police. Even gave them a copy of my hotel receipt."

"Any idea why someone would kill Forester? And in the way they did?"

"I can't speak as to the method, but the motive seems obvious, doesn't it? Randolph Manor. If you are looking for someone with motive, I suggest you speak with that snake in the grass Victor Hamilton."

I thanked Raintree for his time and exited the store. At the small bridge I paused to study my reflection in the goldfish pond. Dead Lines Books appeared to be doing okay. Customers milled around the cash register. The shelves were orderly and well stocked, baseboards swept clean of spiderwebs. By all indications, the bookstore was surviving.

But I wondered: *How many books does Raintree have to sell each month to pay the rent? Retail lease space can't be cheap, not*

on Main Street. Figure the net profit per book sold is a couple
dollars and he'd have to sell, what? A thousand books a month?
Ten thousand?

I had no idea what sort of income Raintree earned from
selling books. But I couldn't help but wonder if serving as head
of a nonprofit would provide Raintree with a nice salary—
maybe a very large one. Which made me wonder: What would
Raintree do for another shot at the Randolph estate? Would
he go so far as to kill Forester? And if so, who better suited to
make Forester's death look like a vampire slaying than a man
selling books on witches, potions, and deadly curses? I decided
the one person best suited to answer that question would be
the man in charge of the murder investigation.

I pulled out my map and located the police station. Folding
the map, I tucked it in my back pocket and started down the
sidewalk toward the Red Wolf Gallery to meet Aunt Vivian.

CHAPTER SIX
DEADLY GAMES

Google 'Dead Lines Books' and see what comes up."

We sat outside a coffee shop on Main Street. I'd met Aunt Vivian at the Red Wolf Gallery, picked up Meg at the coroner's office, and swung by her house so she could get her laptop. Now the three of us sat huddled around a table sipping coffee and discussing the case. Well, actually, Meg and I were discussing the case. Aunt Vivian was busy with her knitting.

"It's a chemo cap for one of the women in my prayer group," Aunt Vivian explained. "I'm stitching the words of Psalm 23 into the pattern."

Meg hit keys on her laptop and looked over the top of her screen at me. "What makes you think he's lying?"

"Raintree? His eyes. When I asked if he'd killed Forester, he looked up and to the left. That's a pretty good indication he was making up his answer. If he'd looked to the right, it would have indicated he was trying to remember something."

"Is this what you're after?" Meg spun the laptop so I could see the screen.

I scooted my chair around the table and studied the bookstore's website.

Our paranormal section is designed to help you find books related to your specific vampire reading interests. For example, we have vampire books for children, young adults, and adults. We also have a section dedicated to Dracula, plus historical novels, urban fantasy, and, of course, romance.

At the bottom of the page was a row of icons for sponsors. Pointing to a button of a gothic mansion, I said, "Click that one."

Another browser window opened, bringing up a new page for THE FULL MOON VAMPIRE SLAYER GAME. At the top of the game's web page was a black-and-white picture of Randolph Manor. Meg and I read silently, scrolling down every few seconds to study the gruesome images.

Finally she said, "Seriously? Who would pay that kind of money to chase a vampire around a spooky mansion?"

"Judging from the customer comments, lots of people. Told you Raintree was hiding something. When I asked if he knew anything about the manor, he told me no. But obviously he knows something if he's willing to link to this game's site from his bookstore page. Click on the Frequently Asked Questions tab."

Under a banner offering "half-off Tuesdays" were the game's pricing levels. *Five hundred dollars for a single player staying overnight in Transylvania's Randolph Manor.* There was a button to click for reservations. *When you arrive you will be greeted by Dr. Barlow, vampirologist and innkeeper of the Randolph Manor.* A description of the accommodations showed pictures of the inside of the manor and even an image of the canopied bed I'd slept in the night before! Under the player's equipment section was a medical bag similar to the one Barlow had given me.

The player's ranking page showed a list of FULL MOON ULTIMATE VAMPIRE SLAYERS. Head shots featured "failed and felled" players, most with bloody mouths and bite marks on their necks. The "About Us" page displayed a picture of the "Dark Coven Master."

"That's Forester," I said. "Even dead I can see the resemblance. Knowing that Barlow, the guesthouse, and Randolph Manor are tied together helps with the case."

Meg said, "It does?"

"Well, sure. Here's how the virtual games work online. There's an innkeeper who welcomes the players and gets them settled in for the game. Inside the castle is a Lord or King or, in this case, the Dark Coven Master. The object of the game is to combat demons and dragons, escape mazes and dungeons, and capture weapons and prizes until finally you confront the head bad guy."

"But you're not talking in real life, just as a game?"

"Right. D&D online gaming is huge. Except with what we're looking at here, the game isn't virtual; it's real. You want to know what I think? I think the game got out of hand and someone accidentally killed Forester. Or maybe Raintree really did kill Forester in order to get the estate. I'll know more in a few minutes."

"What are you doing now?" Meg asked me.

"Sending my editor a text message asking him to send me the IP address of the form submission that tipped us off to the case. If I can trace the address, I can find out where the sender was when he or she filled out the form."

After sending the message, I put my phone away and pulled Meg's laptop toward me. "Mind if I drive? There's something I need to check."

I typed in the URL for my group's TV Crime Watchers website. When the log-in screen appeared, I entered my ID and password.

Meg said, "And now?"

"Pulling up our database of television shows." I typed in key words like *haunted*, *spooky*, *ghosts*, *vampires*, and *séances*. "If there has ever been a television show featuring a haunted house as a plot element, I'll find it."

"But I thought you just said Forester died because of a game that got out of hand."

"That's one theory, sure. And probably what happened, but to be sure ..."

The screen refreshed and a list of popular crime shows popped up on the screen: *CID, CSI, FBI, JAG, NCIS.*

"But those are all legal shows," said Meg.

"Sorts uppercase first."

More shows appeared: *Colombo, Dead Like Me, Deadly Bones, Ghost Whisperer, Magnum PI, Matlock, McCloud Monk, Kojak, Paranormal Witness, Rockford Files, Six Feet Under, The Mentalist...*

"How many in your database?"

"Hundreds."

"And you've watched them all?"

"Not all. But we're constantly adding members to our group, so someone watched and loaded the synopsis into the system. Now I'm going to refine my search of the episodes to ones that only feature paranormal murders."

"How long will *that* take?"

"Awhile." Opening a second browser window, I asked, "Want to see where I work?"

The *Cool Ghoul Gazette* website popped up.

Meg pointed to one of the tabs on the page and asked, "Breaking Noose?"

"That was my editor's idea. Here, let's see what's happening in the world of the weird and paranormal."

I clicked on the button and a Breaking Noose article appeared.

The headline at the top of the page read GOAT MAN
SPOTTED IN WYOMING MOUNTAINS:

> Local law enforcement agents report that a man hiking
> near Big Sky Peak spotted a person dressed like a goat
> among a herd of sheep. "A couple of hunters heard what
> they thought was an animal in distress," officer Barry Cade
> said. "But it turned out to be a man in a dress wearing
> goat horns."

"Seriously? That's news?" Meg asked.

"Over nine thousand eyeballs." I tapped the eyeball icon at
the bottom of the story. "Somebody found it interesting."

I scrolled down to the next article.

It read:

> FURRY SHOPLIFTER "BEARLY" ESCAPES—A three-
> hundred-pound black bear surprised shoppers at a
> Blacksburg, Virginia, convenience store this past weekend
> when the animal pushed open the automatic doors and
> ambled over to the snack rack. Security guards chased
> the bear from the store but not before the hungry female
> snagged a box of peanut brittle and a case of Moon Pies.

"I like Moon Pies."

"Me too," I replied, "but not enough to fight a bear for
them. Ah, here's one in my area of interest."

> GEORGIA FUNERAL HOME ADDS COFFEE BAR—Jenson
> Funeral Home began serving coffee to its mourners.

"When you're standing in line and waiting to pay your respects, you have a lot of dead time on your hands," funeral home owner Bill Jenson reported. "Adding a coffee bar makes sense. We've already seen an uptick in foot traffic and picked up several new clients."

I checked the progress bar of the search results. It continued to creep along.

"This might take longer than I thought." To Aunt Vivian I said, "Is there a particular time you need to be back to your facility?"

"I'm the one paying to stay at the center, child. I can come and go as I wish. Why?"

"I'd like to see the crime scene. Any chance you can run me up to the golf resort?"

"I'll need a nap first. Not as young as I once was."

"We have a spare bedroom," Meg said. "You're welcome to it."

"Bless you."

"How about you?" Meg said to me. "Do you need a nap too?"

"Look at you being sarcastic. No, I'll go ask the police what they have to say about this case."

CHAPTER SEVEN
HEAD COUNT, ONE MISSING

Lieutenant Ralph McAlhany worked out of an old gymnasium at the end of Main Street. I announced my arrival at the receptionist's window and explained I was an investigative reporter covering the death of Barnabas Forester. She studied my business card and directed me toward a wooden bench that looked as if it had seen lots of use on a football field.

Fresh green paint coated cinder-block walls, and the entranceway had recently been carpeted and smelled of glue. The police station had the feel of one of the modular units at my school — refurbished and functional and out of place among the other office buildings on Main Street.

I hunched forward on the bench and clicked off the three things I needed for the story: a picture of the body, a list of people connected to Forester, and a look at the murder weapon. Knowing that Randolph Manor might have been connected to the vampire slaying game helped put things into perspective. If Forester were a recluse, like Raintree said, and involved in the game, then he'd need a front person for marketing, and who better than Raintree? The bookstore owner appeared business savvy. The challenge now was to track down a list of recent players and get a look at the murder weapon.

I'd been waiting maybe ten minutes when the receptionist tapped the window and pointed toward a female officer. I followed her through double doors and onto the basketball court, which was portioned off into a maze of cubicles. We made our way down a hallway and past an old equipment cage. The lieutenant's office was in a locker room.

Lieutenant Ralph McAlhany was a broad-shouldered man with dark glossy hair, high cheekbones, and dark, almond-shaped eyes. His brown shirt and slacks were pressed and creased and screamed professionalism. He waved me into the cage while he remained on the phone, listening. Judging from his expression, the call was not going well. He pointed to a chair and I sat.

The call ended and he looked across the desk. "That was the mayor's office telling me it'll be another six weeks before they can break ground on our new law enforcement center. We were supposed to be in our new building last winter, but our funding got cut at the state level so here we are." McAlhany aimed his coal-black eyes at me and said, "What can I do for you?"

I passed him one of my *Cool Ghoul Gazette* business cards. The lieutenant studied the front, then turned it over. His eyebrows arched when he read the note from the marshal of Deadwood.

"Deadwood Canyon. I think I remember something about that case. The ghost town murder that wasn't, then was. The way I heard it, a boy identified the killer by watching TV."

"I compare evidence against police and detective shows," I said, trying to sound calmer than I was.

Dad had warned me to stay out of trouble and keep my mouth in check, and here I was sitting across from the one guy who could lock me up if I said the wrong thing.

"After I analyze the shows that best fit the crime, I tell the authorities who I think committed the murder. Or try to. Most don't respond to my emails or calls. It helps to watch a lot of TV."

"I know a few of my officers who might be candidates for that type of work. Can't keep them off their smartphones long enough to do their jobs."

"I'd be happy to give them a demonstration, if you like."

I couldn't tell if he was making fun of me or truly interested in my work, so I kicked the conversation in a different direction.

"McAlhany? Is that Irish?"

He chuckled. "I know. The hair and eyes throw people off. My mother was a full-blooded Cherokee. She worked most of her life at the casino outside Waynesville and wanted more for her son than reservation work and working the tourist trade. Married my father when she was in her thirties. He was an ex-New York cop, pushing fifty. Spent his whole life in New York's 114th Precinct. Died of a heart attack my sophomore year at Notre Dame. But you didn't come by to hear my story."

I shifted uneasily in my chair. "Any thoughts on who might want Mr. Forester dead?"

"Get to the point much quicker and that sergeant who brought you here won't have time to finish running the background check on you. Orlando, was it? On a trip with your family?"

"Yes, sir."

We were dancing. He was enjoying it more than I was.

"You know I can't comment about the case. It's an ongoing investigation. Not even allowed to confirm if there *is* an investigation. I'm only speaking with you because earlier today your aunt dropped off a platter of sugar cakes. She's a right persuasive woman, your aunt."

Good old Aunt Vivian was fast becoming my favorite relative.

"But Forester *is* dead. And somebody killed him."

"Fact is, we haven't ruled it a homicide yet. Might have died of natural causes. The chest wound could have come after he was dead, which would make it a whole different kind of crime. Look, I know you'd love for this to turn out to be one of those gruesome horror stories that gets spread across the Web. Bet that'd make the editor of your little website real happy. That is why you're here, right? For a story? But until I know more, all we have is a dead man on a golf course with cause of death undetermined. Fact is, dying during a round of golf isn't all that strange."

"But getting stabbed with a wooden stake is. Did you know Forester was part of a vampire role-playing game?"

"I heard something about that. Never have understood this infatuation with vampires and zombies. It's like people today are searching for evidence of ghosts and monsters while at the same time rejecting any notion of God. I'm not saying I'm a religious man. Being raised both Catholic and Cherokee made for some pretty strange discussions in our home. But I've never seen anything like what's going on today. You a believer?"

"Believer in what, vampires?"

"God. I'm asking because it seems to me a boy your age coming in here asking all these questions about vampires might be looking for something other than information about one man's death."

All this God business made me uncomfortable, so I steered the conversation back to the case. "Mind if I read you something?"

"You know it's okay, right? To believe? Most everyone does."

I held up the vampire mythology book I'd found in my

room. "Found this by my bed last night. Mind if I read you something?"

"Why not? All we're doing is wasting time."

"'Although Europe experienced an outbreak of the Black Plague in the sixth century, the disease lay dormant until 1320, when a pandemic developed in the Gobi Desert. It spread and decimated populations across the globe. The Black Death reached Europe in the mid–fourteenth century and resurfaced regularly throughout the next couple hundred years. The sheer number of deaths meant communal graves had to be reopened regularly. At the time, little was known about the process of human decomposition. The grotesque appearance of decomposing corpses led some to believe that the bodies were being reanimated. Meanwhile, symptoms of the Black Plague often appeared as tumors on the neck that burst open and bled. Later, victims would often vomit blood.'"

"What are you driving at, son?"

"What we're seeing today with vampires isn't all that new. People have been freaking out over this stuff for decades."

"Only proves people today who believe in vampires aren't any smarter than they were back then."

"By chance do you have a list of players who might have participated in the vampire slayer game? I'm sure that's a lead you're looking into."

"We're holding off on that until we see what the autopsy report says."

"But that could take days."

"Time is the one thing I have lots of. What I don't have is enough resources to track down every harebrained idea."

It seemed to me that McAlhany wasn't nearly as anxious to catch the killer as I was.

"Who discovered the body?"

"Groundskeeper."

"Which hole?"

"Thirteen. If you think that bit of information will be of interest to your readers, you might want to mention that it's a dogleg par four. Plays longer than the yardage due to the narrow fairway and the sharp drop-off next to the out-of-bounds area."

"Any thoughts on the victim's strange dental work?"

"You mean the fangs? Glued on, obviously. But I can't say conclusively because . . ."

"I know. It's an ongoing investigation."

"I was going to say, until the oral surgeon arrives and delivers her findings. Leave me your number and I'll call you once I know something definitive. How's that for helping a struggling reporter?"

I forced a smile, mumbling, "Thanks."

I imagined myself in the lieutenant's position, trying to do a job and working out of a boys' locker room with some fourteen-year-old kid asking lame questions about a dead man dressed up like a vampire.

I said, "Ever seen the movie *Rampage*?"

"Can't say I have."

"Released in the late eighties. It's based on the case of

Richard Chase, the so-called Vampire of Sacramento. Chase was a deeply disturbed young man who injected rabbit's blood into his veins. They had him committed to a mental institution. He'd only been in the facility a few days when they found him with blood all over his face and in his mouth. Turns out he'd built a bird feeder and was catching sparrows and drinking their blood. Staff began referring to him as Dracula. Hospital doctors diagnosed him as a paranoid schizophrenic and treated him with psychotropic drugs. After a few months they pronounced him cured and released him into the care of his mother, but she didn't like her son being doped up all the time so she took him off his meds. Chase killed six people before they captured him. He never bit anybody's neck, though."

"This isn't what we have here."

"How can you be sure?"

"Even if Forester was going around acting like a vampire and biting people's necks, I can't imagine anyone actually killing him with a wooden stake. Sure, someone might call a tabloid news reporter, but commit murder? I don't see it."

"Have there been any reports of vandals digging up graves? Opening caskets? Looking into old burial grounds, that sort of thing?"

"Sounds to me like you've been talking to Phillip Raintree. If I were you, I'd ignore most of what that man says. Raintree would put up billboards on the Parkway and advertise vampire covens in Transylvania if he thought it would bring people to his store and help him sell books."

"He told me occult books were only a small portion of his business."

"Son, if you believe that malarkey, you'll never make it in journalism. Twice Raintree has been threatened with eviction. Both times he got caught up on his rent payments just before they padlocked the doors. Someone or some organization is keeping him in business. Could be that game you're referring to."

He leaned forward and rested his elbows on the desk. "The fact is, we don't have any evidence tying Raintree or anyone else to Forester's death. I'm not saying Raintree wasn't involved. I am saying it's a stretch to make more of this than there is until we have an official cause of death."

"Suppose Forester *was* into hanging around cemeteries. Getting ideas for his vampire slayer game and scoping out locations. Any idea where he might go?"

"If you're dead set on chasing that rabbit trail, you should check out Skull Creek. That's the Randolph family plot. The way I understand it, Forester moved to Transylvania for his health. Winters here can be harsh, but not like up north. The Randolph Manor came on the market, and Forester put a bid in and bought the place. And as far as this vampire game business goes, around town people think it's a joke."

I was tempted to tell the lieutenant that the vampire slayer "game" scared the mess out of me. Instead I asked what the victim had been wearing. Maybe I could get a decent quote from that.

"I suppose there's no harm in telling you. Black cape, black slacks, white shirt."

"And the murder weapon? Any chance I could take a look?"

Please, please, please!

He shook his head. "Part of an ongoing ..."

"Investigation. Got it."

McAlhany rose from his chair, signaling the conversation was over. He walked around the desk and rested his hip on the corner.

"Mind if I give you some career advice, son? Don't make more of this story than it is. I met the marshal of Deadwood at a conference a few years back. Seemed like a straight-up lawman. Can't say working in a ghost town is my idea of real police work, but it's not my place to judge another man's vocation. That's why it's a shame about what happened with your suspect out there."

"What do you mean? We caught him."

A look of genuine concern came over his face. "I'm sorry, I thought you'd heard. Your lead suspect hired himself a top-shelf lawyer and got himself released on bail, then jumped. Last I heard he was still on the loose."

"He's gone?"

"Like the wind."

I slumped in my chair. I'd worked hard to solve that case, and now to think the killer might never stand trial ... "I appreciate you taking time to talk with me, Lieutenant, I do."

I started to stand, but he put his hand on my shoulder and kept me seated.

"People in Transylvania, we like our solitude. That's why

my father came down from New York, to get away from crack-pots and criminals. We can't change the name of our town, at least not without going to a lot of trouble. But you'd better believe we can do something about what people think of us. If I hear that you're making Transylvania look like something it's not, then I don't care how sweet your aunt is—you'll have me to deal with. Are we clear?"

"Yes, sir."

"Thing is, you say *murder* and people go, 'What? Where?' Then after a few days they forget about it. You say *vampire* and I've got every news outlet in the country calling me. You get what I'm saying?"

"I think so, sure."

"Good. Then we should get along just fine." He released his grip on my shoulder and walked me into the hallway.

I took a few steps, turned, and asked, "By chance, do you happen to have a picture of the deceased?"

"I wish I could, but ..."

"It's part of an ongoing investigation."

He winked. "If I hear anything from the oral surgeon, I'll call. I have your number," he said, thumping my business card against his knuckles.

"Thanks again for your time, Lieutenant."

I worked my way back through the maze of cubicles in the gymnasium and out the front door. Standing on the front steps in the blinding white sunshine, I realized that nearly twenty-four hours earlier I'd been sitting in the Brown Derby with my parents, trying to convince them to let me come to Transylvania. Now I stood neck deep in a murder investigation involving a vampire — or at least someone pretending to be a vampire — and I still did not have a solid lead on who had killed Forester and why.

On top of that, the one case I had solved might not even matter because some judge let the killer out on bail. Things definitely weren't going my way. Just then my phone buzzed.

"Nick, oh my gosh, I can't believe it. Something's happened."

The voice sounded on the edge of panic.

"Meg?" My mind went immediately to Aunt Vivian. "What is it?"

"When I got back from lunch I found the door to the morgue standing wide open and the fridge we use to store blood samples cleaned out! Nick, Forester's body is gone! I think our dead vampire escaped!"

CHAPTER EIGHT
DEATH THREAT

I'm a pretty fast runner. I know my parents think all I do is lounge around and watch movies and videos on my computer, but during commercials I do push-ups. Twenty reps if it's a long one. And at least three times a week I sprint a mile. Not the whole mile, obviously. I mean, that would kill me. But I leg it out pretty good. I have no idea what my time is, but I'm no slouch. I've watched too many cop shows where the fat detective can't catch the bad guy ... or escape from him, and I don't want to be dead like the dude on TV.

Good thing, because as soon as I hung up from talking to Meg, I cut down an alleyway to get over to her street. I'd only gone a few steps when I heard movement behind me. Whirling, I got my arm up just as someone clubbed me above the ear. The blow sent me sprawling face-first onto the pavement, and before I could fight back, a forearm clamped under my throat and wrenched my neck sideways in a choke hold.

"You think this is a game?" the voice hissed in my left ear. "You think this is one of your television cop shows? I could kill you now, but where is the fun in that?"

Oven-hot breath blew across my neck; fingernails clawed at my windpipe. I tried to wiggle out of his grasp, but squirming only caused the arm to clamp down tighter.

"You're so smart, so clever with all your questions and poking around where you shouldn't. Can you guess what comes next? No? Let me give you a hint." The voice fell to a whisper. "The monster you seek feeds at dusk and preys on the flesh of young women."

"Please, can't ... breathe."

"Leave now while you still can."

I clenched my left fist and brought it up over my shoulder as hard as I could, but the blow only thumped weakly off a muscled shoulder and fell away. The assailant struck back by slamming an elbow into my temple and planting my face into the pavement. As quickly as he'd pounced, he released me and darted back into the shadows, his dark, silky cape fluttering behind the dumpster. I balanced myself on knees and knuckles and, taking a final look behind me, sprinted from the alley like a runner coming out of the blocks.

I was still running, still checking to make sure I wasn't being followed, when a front bumper clubbed me on the thigh and sent me somersaulting into the air. The impact bounced me off the windshield and over the roof. I landed in the street and heard tires screeching.

☠

"He just came out of nowhere, ran right in front of my car."

A middle-aged woman bent down, her face contorted with worry as she leaned over me. Next to her, a heavyset man in a blue work shirt knelt on one knee. I tried to sit up, but he put his hand on my shoulder.

"Don't move, son. An ambulance is on the way."

The man's voice reverberated off the walls of my head, booming like a football stadium loudspeaker. The edges of my vision appeared too bright, and voices seemed loud and close.

I levered myself into a sitting position and brushed the man's hand from my shoulder. I noticed I'd tomahawked skin off three knuckles. I wiped my hand across my jeans and got up, massaging my thigh.

"Hey, kid, you need to sit back down and wait for the ambulance."

I wobbled back toward the alley, saw it was empty, and limped off toward Meg's.

With each step the throbbing in my thigh lessened. The thing was, except for skinned knees and knuckles and a dull ringing in my head, I really was okay. A split second before the car hit me, I'd jumped and turned the collision into an aerial flip, just like I'd done countless times before while snowboarding. Smacking the windshield and falling onto the pavement hadn't hurt nearly as much as landing on packed snow after missing a half-pipe jump.

So yeah, other than almost getting flattened by a pickup and being mugged in the alley, I was fine.

Meg was still in her blue scrubs and green Crocs when I walked onto the front steps of her house.

"What happened to *you*?"

"Took a fall."

"I'll say. Sit while I get something for your hand. I can't have you bleeding all over Mom's porch."

Meg returned moments later with a wad of paper towels. I could tell the missing corpse had left her shaken because when I asked if I could borrow her laptop to write a teaser for my *Cool Ghoul Gazette* article, she numbly agreed. While she went back inside to get bandages and antiseptic for my hand, I banged out a short piece with all the pertinent details, including the fact that our victim—the one with fangs, bite marks, and a gaping hole in his chest—had gone AWOL. I deliberately left out the business of the mugging, because I didn't want my editor or Aunt Vivian to worry. And I especially didn't want to alarm Meg.

I hit the send button and said to Meg, "Can't believe you lost the body."

"I didn't lose it. Someone took it—that's the only explanation."

She pressed a bandage against my knuckles. Her hands felt soft and warm and I noticed she smelled like oranges. There was something oddly comforting about the way she dressed the wound, a special tenderness that made me think she didn't really think I was as obnoxious as she'd said.

"You did lock up, right?"

She rolled her eyes and sighed, sending a wave of warm minty breath my direction.

"What do you think? Yes, I locked up, I'm sure of it." She tucked a strand of hair behind her ear. "I don't know what I'm going to do if it turns out this was my fault."

"Maybe the oral surgeon took the body," I offered. "Or your boss had it shipped off for an autopsy."

She pursed her lips and squeezed the bandage onto the last scrape.

"Sure, I thought about that. But why would someone take blood samples? Doesn't make sense."

"Maybe Forester needed a snack."

"That's not funny."

"You're the one who said our vampire had escaped. I'm just going along with the story. Who else knows about this besides us?"

"I left a message on Dr. Edwards's cell. He only works part-time at the morgue. His real job is keeping the books at a local car dealership. This is awful, just awful."

"Maybe we should ask the lieutenant to put out a bolo. You know, a 'be on the lookout' for a walking corpse."

"Really, you can stop with the jokes now."

Aunt Vivian pushed open the screen door and stepped onto the porch.

"Mercy me, we lost another one."

"Forester isn't lost," Meg shot back. "It's just that *I* don't know where he is."

"Oh? Did something happen to our victim?"

"I thought that's what we were talking about," Meg replied.

"Heavens no, child. I'm talking about my neighbor across the hall, Lila May. The retirement center likes for me to check in every couple of hours to make sure nothing's happened. Like I can't be trusted to spend a day with my great-nephew. But I suppose it's understandable. We do seem to get lost a lot. Why, just last week we went to the mall and got lost coming home. Thought they'd never find us. Anyhow, I called to let them know I'd be gone the rest of the day, and they told me Lila May keeled over during that show, *One-Minute Makeup.* Bless her heart. One minute Lila May is watching a segment on belly-blasting supplements and the next she's standing before her Maker."

"Anything I can do?" I asked.

"Find a cure for aging."

I winked at Meg and said, "You need to check with Barnabas Forester on that."

Vertical lines creased Meg's brow. "Sure, make fun, go on. This is all your fault."

"My fault?"

"Yes. If you hadn't insisted on seeing the body, none of this might have happened."

"Look at you two. Squabbling like an old married couple." Aunt Vivian eased over and looked down at my hand. "Goodness me, what happened?"

"It's nothing."

"He fell," Meg said. "Probably because he was jumping to conclusions."

"Now look who's making a funny."

"Aunt Vivian, please don't mention this to anyone," Meg said. "My mom helped me get that job at the morgue. If I mess up even a little, it could look bad on my college application."

"Don't worry, child. I lose things all the time. Why, last week I was in the checkout line at Ingles. I had two sympathy cards and a picture frame for one of the ladies on our wing. And when I went to pay, I couldn't find my wallet. I emptied my purse on the counter trying to find it, which was embarrassing. But the kicker was when the woman behind me said, 'Is that your wallet under your arm?'"

Pretending to peek under Meg's elbow, I said, "Nope, Forester isn't there."

"Ha-ha," Meg replied dryly. "You're *sooooo* funny."

"Hey, I have an idea," said Aunt Vivian. "Let's pray!"

"For a corpse?" I asked.

"For Meg. Let's pray she doesn't get in trouble with her boss."

"I'm sure it will be fine," Meg said. "I'm sure there is a logical explanation for what happened to the body." Meg manufactured a smile. "One that *doesn't* involve a zombie-like body on the loose."

But I wasn't 100 percent sure. The scene in the alley still had me spooked, if not downright scared. Not that I would admit it. Mom is always after me to share my feelings, to "open up." Why moms and girls *feel* it's important for boys to talk about their raw emotions is as big a mystery as some of the murders I've watched on TV. Only thing I can figure is they're wired differently. "Haywired" is what my buddy Tommy calls it.

I never see Dad act scared, even when I know he probably is. He gets mad, sure. And he'll laugh at funny television commercials and some of the same movies I watch. That's emotion, right? Mom and Wendy almost never laugh at the movies we watch. But let a sappy love story come on and it's tissues and tears all over the place. Only time I ever saw Dad cry was when he watched that baseball movie *Field of Dreams*. I think he missed playing catch with his own dad.

So yeah, I was scared that someone popped me in the alley, but you know what? Boys my age are getting mugged and shot at all the time, so it's not like what happened to me was anything special.

"Where are you going?" Meg asked me.

"To see the widow. Maybe she can tell me who would want her husband dead."

CHAPTER NINE
PORTRAIT OF A KILLER

Lucy Forester lived in a bungalow tucked behind a hedge shaped like a dragon. The placard stuck into the ground informed me the bush was wintergreen boxwood. In fact, each plant, bush, and tree carried an identifying placard, all hand painted and tipped with calligraphy. The dragon's open mouth and fangs formed one half of an archway, its spiked tail the other.

I followed the pebble walkway through a flower garden decorated with brightly colored ceramic gnomes peeping out from behind ferns. Pinwheels whirled with the breeze; flute music played through a speaker near a fountain. It occurred to me that Lucy might be the inspiration behind the garden design at Dead Lines Books and, if so, may also be connected to the vampire slayer game.

As I started up the front steps, I heard yelling coming from around the side of the house. Moments later a man came backing toward me with his hands up. Chasing him across the yard was a woman wielding a garden hoe and wearing a yellow T-shirt under bib overalls.

"I'll burn Randolph Manor down before selling to you!" she yelled at the man.

"Crazy broad, have you lost your mind?"

She swung the hoe, almost taking off his head. He stumbled backward, tripped over lawn ornaments, and went hurrying toward a black Escalade parked on the street.

"You'd better run!" she called after him.

Pausing by the driver's door he yelled back, "Lady, you need help!"

The SUV sped away, and I wheeled back around and lifted my hands in a defensive posture.

"If you're selling magazine subscriptions or with a church, keep walking."

I moved sideways to put the water fountain between us. "Mind if I ask you a few questions about your husband's death?"

"Oh geez. Not another one. Why won't you people leave me alone?" She lowered the hoe, resting it on her shoulder. Cocking her head, she asked, "Aren't you a little young to be a reporter?"

I told her about the *Cool Ghoul Gazette* and the sort of stories we ran.

"If you want to talk, we'll have to do it while I work. I'm in the middle of a project."

I followed Lucy Forester into the backyard and inside a cedar-plank work shed sitting in the corner of the lot. Empty portrait frames hung on faded gray walls; the smell of paint and cleaning solvents filled the air. Lucy Forester pushed a tabby cat off a three-legged stool and sat, hooking her toes over the bottom rung. Sprigs of blonde hair sprouted from beneath a pink ball cap. Her dimpled cheeks were tanned and smooth and flecked with paint speckles.

At a certain age boys start noticing things. I found myself staring at Forester's widow and thinking: *She's really, really pretty.*

I leaned against the windowsill and hooked one foot over the other. "Who's the man who just left?"

"Victor Hamilton. If you're a reporter, I would think you've already interviewed him."

"Hamilton owns the golf resort, right?"

"Not outright. He's more like the managing partner with a substantial interest."

She selected a brush and began moving slender fingers across the canvas of a partially painted landscape.

"I was going to interview him next," I said.

"If you know about Barry's purchase of the estate, then you also know why I would never sell the property to Hamilton. Not that it's mine to sell. Living with Barry in that dreary little house by the creek was one of the low points in my life. You cannot imagine how depressing it is to run a bed-and-breakfast with a man who loathes people. But our couple's counselor said we needed to work through our differences and having a common goal and project would help. It did not."

"What did you mean about the estate not being yours to sell?"

"You ever done mission work?"

"No, ma'am. I mean, sometimes for school I do community service, sure. It's a graduation requirement now. Why?"

"It's a cliché, people say it all the time, but it's true. Seeing how the rest of the world lives really makes you appreciate where you're from. Americans are spoiled and selfish, and most of us wouldn't last a day living on what a child in Nicaragua lives on in a month. You want to learn to appreciate what you have, spend some time in La Chureca. That's the city dump outside Managua. The 'Churequeros' make homes out of trash. Every day they search for scraps of plastic and glass to sell for money. That's their only source of income. There is an elementary school located on the dump, but once kids graduate, most just stay in the dump, scrounging for scraps. Seeing the faces of children when they put on their first new pair of shoes and walk out of that dump into a new life—now that's priceless."

She tucked the tip of her tongue in the corner of her mouth and concentrated on the painting. For a few seconds I wasn't sure if she had forgotten my question or not. Finally, she put the brush aside and studied me with intense blue eyes.

"Barry came from money, lots of it, and he insisted on a prenuptial agreement. He bought the Randolph estate with his money. Obviously, since we'd filed for divorce, he wasn't going to leave me the estate. But even if the Randolph estate were mine, I'd never sell it to someone like Hamilton. Not after what he did to the other side of the mountain."

"So you don't inherit anything?"

"Not even life insurance. Barry didn't believe in it." She stopped and looked at me curiously. "I thought you told me you were writing an article for a vampire site."

"The reporting job is just part of the reason I'm here. Solving murders is sort of a hobby of mine."

"How cute, a boy your age catching killers."

She picked up another brush and started in a different corner of the painting.

"I loved my husband. Put that in your story. I know people enjoy talking about things that aren't any of their business, especially in this town, but the truth is Barry and I had a complicated relationship. One that led to some outlandish rumors."

I wondered why she wasn't more upset over her husband's death. Even if they had filed for divorce, she must've loved him at some point. Was she so emotionally unattached she didn't care anymore? And if so, did that make her a cold-blooded murderer? Or was she just putting up a wall for nosy people like me?

I said, "You don't seem too upset about his death."

"Everyone grieves in different ways. I paint." She switched

to another brush and hitched herself closer to the easel. "Aren't you going to ask me if I killed my husband?"

"Did you?"

"No. I was home that evening. In fact, I haven't left the house all week except to walk down to the cooperative to get some fresh vegetables."

"Can anyone confirm that?"

She feigned surprise. "Oh my, do I need an alibi? Should I get a lawyer?" Her mocking smile caught me off guard. "Don't worry, I'm just giving you a hard time. I've been through all this with the lieutenant. My car is in the shop, something to do with the catalytic converter. Been there all week. If they can get it fixed, I plan to sell it. Cars are killing the planet." She stroked the tabby with her bare foot. "To answer your question, no, I was home alone with my cats the night Barry died. As I am most nights."

"Any thoughts on the weird circumstances surrounding your husband's death?"

"You mean why was he dressed like a vampire? I honestly have no idea. Barry suffered from a physical disorder called XP. That's a disease that prevents him from spending time in the sun. XP is a recessive genetic disorder of DNA that prohibits the body from repairing skin damage caused by ultraviolet light. Those who have it are at a higher risk for developing melanoma."

"Sort of like porphyria?" I could tell from her reaction she'd never heard of it. "It's blood-related and leads to rapid skin deterioration. It leaves the victim with a ghastly pallor and enlarged teeth due to gum damage. Any sunlight, even for a few minutes, causes the skin to blister and burn. Back before people knew better, they thought drinking blood could reverse its effects. It's part of the mythology surrounding vampires and why they can't be in the sun."

"It wasn't like Barry couldn't be outside at *all*. Just between you and me, I think he liked it when people gossiped. But his physical problems were minor compared to the psychological ones."

"Oh?"

"Barry and I were polar opposites. I'm a California beach girl; Barry grew up in upstate New York. I'm sure you noticed the arrangement of flora when you arrived. Blue sky and sunshine and being around other people: these are my channels of energy. Barry hated crowds. When I wasn't home, he'd draw the blinds and sit in the dark."

"Is that why you two split up?"

She readjusted the easel to catch more of the afternoon light coming through the rear window. The portrait was coming along fine—a violent orange sunset behind purple mountains. In the foreground was a gray wolf with hungry yellow eyes.

"Opposites attract, but that doesn't always make for a good marriage. Funny thing is, we moved here from New York because I thought the change in climate would help."

"So you two are not long-time residents?"

"Hardly. Took me awhile to convince Barry to move, but

once he found that mansion up on the mountain, he agreed. As I said, he's set in his ways. I'd hoped he might take up hiking. Or biking. Anything to get him out of the house. I'm a hopeless romantic and a terrible businesswoman. We turned the guesthouse into a B&B, but we never had the first guest, thank goodness. Can you hand me that rag?"

She cleaned paint from her hands and handed it back to me.

"Did you know your husband was involved in a vampire gaming website?"

"Barry?" she said, chuckling. "He could barely turn on a computer, much less navigate the Internet. If I were you, I'd go back and check my source on that one."

I let the comment pass. Could be she really didn't know what went on up in the manor. "How about you? Do you have a website for your gallery?"

"There is a man in town, a friend, sort of. He helps me make changes to my blog. I can't even remember my password."

"So your husband never mentioned visiting graveyards or poking around crypts? That sort of thing?"

"Barry loved books. He was engrossed in them, all kinds. That was the world he roamed. No, to my knowledge Barry never visited any graveyards."

She put her brush down, stretched, and worked her neck side to side, releasing the tension.

"Look, my husband was not a monster or freak. Just a very sad man."

"Who is dead."

"Please, you needn't remind me."

"I'm just saying, he had something someone wanted."

"I cannot imagine what. As I said, there was no insurance money. The estate goes to a nonprofit. Or at least, I think it does. Barry was in the process of amending his will ... again. He did that quite often."

"Do you happen to know which nonprofit he named in his will?"

"I think he mentioned something about a wildlife preserving group, but I could be wrong about that. Now, then, I have this painting to finish. The gallery is expecting it for this weekend's showing. We're doing a private affair for some New York buyers."

I studied the portrait of the oversized wolf with its hollow cheeks and hungry eyes, and wondered if Lucy Forester had studied the wolf dog and memorized its terrorizing bulk and features. I thanked her for her time and mentioned I might stop back by later.

"Not to chat," I explained, "but so my aunt can see your work."

"The gallery in town would be the best place for that."

I told her I could find my way out and left.

The widow certainly *seemed* pleasant enough. She was amiable and transparent, a California beach girl with a "live and let live" attitude. She expressed none of the nervousness I would have expected from a murderous spouse. Either she was an excellent liar or completely clueless as to the dangerous game being played at the manor.

It occurred to me that if Forester had planned to leave the estate to Raintree's nonprofit and then changed his mind, that would give the bookstore owner a possible motive for murder. Or maybe Forester was in the midst of changing the will so Victor Hamilton could buy the estate. Could be Forester had grown tired of the vampire game idea and just wanted to sell the property so he could move back to New York.

Only way to find out is to visit the scene of the crime and ask Hamilton.

CHAPTER TEN
MURDER AS (AND AT) THE LAST RESORT

Your boss must've shipped the body off to be autopsied," I said. "It's the only plausible explanation." *At least I hope that's the case. Otherwise Forester just might be a vampire and the creature that mugged me in the alley.*

I sat in the backseat of Aunt Vivian's Cadillac, my elbows resting on Meg's front headrest.

"Either Charlotte or Chapel Hill," I said, "and I'm guessing Chapel Hill."

"No way," Meg responded. "If it was on its way to Chapel Hill, Dr. Edwards would have told me. Getting a recommendation from anyone at UNC's medical school would be huge on my college admission application. Dr. Edwards knows I would have begged him to let me ride along."

I let the comment go and turned to another page in *Vampire Mythology: The Curse of Darkness.*

> Another contributing factor to the modern vampire myth is Vlad Tepes, the central figure behind Bram Stoker's Dracula character. Tepes came to power in Wallachia, a part of modern-day Romania, in 1447, and enjoyed a short but brutal reign. He ordered villages destroyed and their residents killed. Impalement was his favorite method of execution. He is rumored to have slaughtered over one hundred thousand people, and according to some scholars, Tepes employed the "stake" as an insult to Christians who have long held that Jesus Christ died in a similar way as punishment for the sins of all humankind.

I closed the journal and said to Meg, "Maybe your boss took the body and he's hiding it in a freezer."

"Are we back to talking about *that*? Why would he do such a thing?"

"Because he could be the killer."

"That's so dumb I'm not even going to comment."

"You just did."

"Did what?"

"Commented."

"I did not," she countered.

"There, you did it again."

"Did what?"

"Commented."

"No, I didn't."

"Would you two lovebirds stop arguing?" said Aunt Vivian. "It's distracting me from driving."

"Think about it, Meg. Who better to cover his tracks and destroy evidence tied to the crime than your boss?"

"But why would Dr. Edwards want to kill Forester?"

"Can't say. Won't know that until I review a summary of the shows that mirror this case."

"So you've already decided Mr. Edwards is the killer?"

"No. I'm only saying he had access to the body. And now that I'm poking around and asking questions, I think I have the killer worried."

"You really do think a lot of yourself."

"Like you don't?"

"Oh, please. You think I'm impressed by *you?*" Meg asked me.

"I meant you think a lot of yourself."

"You know, you two make a great couple," said Vivian. "You remind me of Mr. and Mrs. . . . . Now what was that couple's name? They had a cat called Snickers. An ornery calico that hissed every time I walked past. No, Snickers was their dog. Or was Snickers the name of Helen Copeland's poodle? Wait, couldn't have been, Helen hated animals. Must've been . . . oh, poo, I just missed our exit."

My phone buzzed and I found a text message from Calvin giving me the IP address of the form submission that tipped us off to the vampire murder. Entering the address into an IP lookup website returned the following information: *State/Region—North Carolina, City—Transylvania*. So someone in town *had* tipped off the *Cool Ghoul Gazette* to the murder of Forester. Someone who maybe, quite possibly, wanted us to feature the story on our website. Question was, who and why? I could think of one person: Raintree.

Half a mile later we turned off the main highway and onto a private drive by short stone walls. Crape myrtle shed purple petals onto lush green grass; deer grazed at the edge of a fairway. Across the road, painted white lines marked a golf cart crossing. Aunt Vivian barely slowed as we blew past the guardhouse.

"Look! We're here!" Aunt Vivian announced as she whipped the car into the parking lot. "Meg and I will hit the gift shops while you do whatever it is you need to do to find that man's killer, but don't take too long. It'll be dark soon. Don't want to be out wandering around with a vampire running loose."

The crime scene was a putting green on thirteen. Yellow tape fluttered from pine branches. Tire tracks in matted grass hinted at the route the ambulance had used to drive away. I snapped a few pictures with my phone and wandered down the service road to the maintenance building. Maybe if I spoke to the witness who found the body I could get a better idea of what happened.

A young man in a mousy-gray work shirt and pants saw me coming. Eyeing me cautiously, he gripped the starter cord on a riding mower and yanked hard. The motor spit and hissed and almost caught. Several more tugs left him winded and the odor of gasoline in the air. I casually wandered over.

"Spark plug could be fouled."

Without looking up he gave the cord another tug. "Don't use this one much."

His dark bangs were tangled, greasy, and fell into his eyes. Thick, furry sideburns spread to his jaw. He yanked the cord once more without luck.

"Want me to hold a screwdriver on the plug and wire while you pull?" I asked. "See if it sparks?"

He straightened and tossed his bangs back. He was a big, husky boy, soft around the middle, with crescent sweat stains under his arms.

"What's your name?"

"Nick."

"I'm Henry." Looking over my shoulder he said, "Did you lose your ball or something?"

"No, just looking for someone who might know something about what happened on hole thirteen a couple nights ago. You see anything odd that night? Or the next day?"

"I couldn't help you with anything like that. Couldn't help you at all." With a long, lumbering stride, he walked quickly into the building and started sorting tools on a workbench. "You're not supposed to be down here. Guests are supposed to stay on the course."

"Thing is, the man they found on the course was dressed funny. I thought maybe you might know something."

"You need to leave. I could get into trouble if someone sees you down here talking to me."

He continued putting sockets into their slots, drill bits in their places.

"Don't want that to happen," I said. "I know how important rules can be."

"You'd better know it!"

I suddenly realized who he reminded me of—Bruce. Bruce was a boy in fifth grade who got put into a learning disabled class. Thing was, there wasn't anything wrong with Bruce except that he was a slow reader and stuttered when he got nervous. He defiantly wasn't a "retard," which is what the other kids in the class called him.

"Say, Henry. Mind if I try starting that mower? Would that be all right?"

His eyes moved from me to the mower and back. "Sure. I guess that's okay."

I bent over the mower and scowled as if I were deep in thought. Truth was, I really had no idea how to get a flooded lawn mower started. *My cousin Fred, now, he'd know.* Out of the corner of my eye I saw Henry watching me.

Guessing at the problem, I went to the workbench, found a spark plug socket, a screwdriver, and a wrench, and walked back to the mower. Henry kept moving tools around but with less energy. I pulled the spark plug wire and spat into the cap. Using the flathead screwdriver, I scraped away rust until the sides and bottom of the tiny thimble were shiny. With the socket wrench I removed the plug and cleaned the contact points and put it all back together.

I gave the cord a hard tug and the motor coughed and hiccupped, then roared to life.

"You sure know how to fix things," Henry said, hurrying over. He knocked back the throttle and said to me, "Say, you wanna help me cut? I only gotta do that bank over there."

"Better not. There's probably rules about letting guests use the lawn equipment."

"Hey, you're right! Boy, you are smart. What'd you say your name was?"

"Nick Caden."

"I'm Henry." He thrust out a greasy hand.

"Nice to meet you, Henry. How long have you been working here?"

"Awhile now. I get to go to school a different way because I'm such a good worker. My uncle says a smart boy like me should be thinking about his future. He says cutting grass on a golf course is a really important job, and once I get a little older, I can maybe start my own landscaping business. My uncle Ralph is a real smart man."

Uncle Ralph? "Your uncle, he isn't a police officer, is he?"

"Hey, you know my uncle?"

"We met earlier today. Your uncle and I were talking about ... something. He's the one who told me how you found that thing we cannot talk about. Just curious, what time do you normally get to work?"

"Early. I have to turn on the water for the sprinklers. If I don't turn on the water, the greens get all messed up and guests can't play golf. That's why I don't go to school during the day. My job here is too important."

"I can see that. So when you arrived a couple of days ago, was it still dark out?"

"Only a little bit dark. In the summer I get to ride my scooter. In the winter I can't because it gets icy. I chained my scooter to the light post like always. Why're you asking so many questions?"

"No reason. So you the first one here most mornings?"

"Yep. 'Cept the other day. Mrs. Forester got here before me."

"Mrs. Forester, you sure?"

"Uh-huh. Her car was in the employees' lot. No one is supposed to be in the employees' lot 'cept employees. We have a rule about that."

"You're sure it was her car?"

He nodded his head. "She keeps flowers in the cup holder.

Not plastic ones. Real daisies. She's a nice lady, Mrs. Forester. Did you know she paints pictures? She made me a picture one time. I put it on the wall of my bedroom. That's why she comes up here sometimes, to paint. But Mr. Hamilton, he doesn't like it when she does. That's why she comes early before he gets here. I don't think her painting bothers anybody, though."

"Except Mr. Hamilton."

"Right."

"You positive Mrs. Forester's car was here when you got to work? No chance it was somebody else's car?"

"Oh, it was hers all right. But she left right after I found the … Hey, I told you! I'm not supposed to talk about that!" With his thumb Henry gunned the throttle.

Over the roar of the motor I shouted, "Thanks, Henry. You've been a big help."

Henry aimed the mower at the wide swath of grass on the bank and rode away, his pudgy midsection jiggling.

I felt bad about taking advantage of Henry's childlike innocence, but I needed answers, and though I hadn't exactly come away with a clearer picture of the killer, I did have another piece of the puzzle. Problem was, Henry's account didn't square with Lucy Forester's. If her car was in the shop at the time of the murder, how could it also be at the golf course the morning after her husband was found dead? Maybe all her pretending to need an alibi was just an act. Maybe Lucy Forester was just another pretty woman lying about the murder of her husband in order to inherit his estate before he cut her out of his will.

I also wondered if Henry might have seen more than he remembered. Like, say, someone lurking in the shadows of those pines on hole thirteen. If so, that might make Henry a valuable witness in a murder investigation.

And a possible target for the killer.

At the top of the drive I turned and waved at Henry. He threw up his hand in a casual way and I felt better. If he was still sore at me, he was already beginning to get over it. *Too bad everyone isn't that forgiving,* I thought as I headed toward the clubhouse to meet with Henry's boss, Victor Hamilton.

CHAPTER ELEVEN
DEAD LAST SUSPECT

The front desk clerk told me I would find Victor Hamilton in the Rhododendron Grill. I stopped at the hostess station, scanned the room, and saw him sitting at a table overlooking a putting green. The managing partner of the Last Resort was a lean man with hair going just a little gray. He had on the same pale blue sport shirt, khakis, and loafers I'd seen him wearing at Lucy Forester's. I introduced myself and asked if he could spare a few minutes.

"You look familiar—do I know you?"

"We almost met earlier this afternoon. I was coming to see Mrs. Forester as you were leaving."

"Oh, right. Sorry you had to see that. Don't know what came over Lucy." Smiling, he put out his hand. "I'm Victor Hamilton. What can I do for you?"

"I'm doing a story on the murder of Barnabas Forester. But first I have to ask, any idea why Mrs. Forester chased you off her property like she did?"

Chuckling, he said, "You don't beat around the bush, do you, kid? I like that. Fact is, I honestly don't know what came over Lucy. We've known each other a long time and I've never seen her fly off the handle like that. Can't say as I blame her, though. Losing her husband and all. Tragic. But the way she reacted, you would have thought I killed her husband."

"Did you?"

Still smiling, he narrowed his eyes slightly. "What did you say your name was?"

"Nick Caden. I'm a reporter for the *Cool Ghoul Gazette*."

"Reporter, that's interesting. Perhaps I should get you a copy of our media kit. We received a new batch from the printer's this week. It could be helpful for your story."

"You didn't answer my question."

Hooking an arm over one corner of his chair, he studied me more closely. "Fine, I'll play along with your little game of twenty questions. What possible reason would I have for wanting to kill Barnabas Forester?"

"To get your hands on Randolph Manor. That's why you stopped by Mrs. Forester's."

"Oh sure, I *might* be interested ... at the right price. But not enough to kill someone. Besides, the Randolph estate is not for sale. That's why I stopped by Lucy's place. I wanted to see if she could confirm a rumor. I'd heard Forester might have had a change of heart and amended his will. See, before he died, it was my understanding that he was going to leave the estate to a wildlife conservation group. If you've been digging into his death, then you know what I'm talking about. But from what I'm hearing, he had a change of heart and was going to cut the nonprofit out altogether. Seems to me if you are looking for motive and opportunity, you should be talking with the owner of Dead Lines Books. If anyone stands to gain from Forester's death, it's Phillip Raintree."

"Where were you the night Forester was murdered?"

"His death hasn't been ruled a murder yet. At least, if it has, no one told me. But I get what you're asking. You want to know if I have an alibi."

"Yes, sir."

"I was at home with my wife."

"All night?"

He pulled a silver card case from his pants pocket and jotted a number down on the back of a white business card.

"My wife's name is Nell." He pushed the card toward me. "She'll vouch for my whereabouts. But don't wait too late to call her. She goes to bed around nine. Her chemo treatments take a lot out of her."

I tucked the card away and said, "Did Mr. Forester have

any enemies that you know of? Upset business partners, or anyone who might have a grudge?"

"In all honesty I didn't know much about the man except what I heard from others. And most of that was pure speculation."

"Did you know about the vampire game he was running out of the manor?"

"I had heard something about that. I wondered if the manor was zoned for recreational activity of that nature. I asked a friend on the city council to check. When I found out it wasn't, I thought about making waves but then decided against it. Forester was mentally unstable — anyone could see that. And his wife had just left him. Kicking a man when he's down, that's not my style."

"What is your style, Mr. Hamilton?"

"I gotta tell you, kid, some people might not appreciate you coming across this confident and smug. Might think of you as some kind of know-it-all. But not me. I wish more of the people working for me had your nerve. Being pushy and confident might be a turnoff to some, but it's been my experience those are the individuals who get things done."

Ouch. Mom had warned me I needed to work on my "condescending arrogance," and I thought I had, but I guess not enough.

Hamilton gazed out the window for a long time as if lost in thought before finally saying, "Money. If you're looking for motive, I'd start there."

"Not revenge or greed?"

"Oh sure, it *might* be something like that, but I doubt it."

"Forester, he didn't need your money, though, did he?"

He smiled at me the way a proud father might when his son scores a basket. I got the impression Hamilton enjoyed sparring with me and didn't see me as a threat at all.

"If you are asking if I tried to buy him out after he purchased the manor, yes, I did. I made him a substantial offer, much larger than what he paid for the place, but he turned me down."

Hamilton hunched forward and lowered his voice as if sharing a secret with me. "Look, kid, for the right amount of money, people will do almost anything. And it doesn't even have to be a large amount. Just having the chance to earn a steady paycheck can be reason enough to kill someone. Take that fellow living at the bottom of the mountain in that dilapidated guesthouse."

"You mean Dr. Barlow?"

"Doctor my foot. I've had more medical training than that clown. He calls himself a pathologist, but I know for a fact he's never set foot on the campus of a medical university. The man is a two-bit actor. He had some small parts in the *Dark Shadows* television show back in the seventies. If you ask me, Barlow is trying to pass himself off as an authority on vampires so he can get back to working in Hollywood. Having his name linked to a murder like this — if Forester's death *was* a murder — would give Barlow credibility."

"Are you saying Barlow killed Forester just to pad his résumé?"

"Of course not. What I am saying is, if Forester dropped dead of a heart attack or some other reason and Barlow found out about it, he could easily dress Forester up like a vampire and dump him on the course. Barlow loves being quoted as an expert on vampires. Have you spoken with him?"

"Barlow? Yes, sir."

"Did you use anything he said in your story?"

"A little. He has some interesting thoughts on how all this vampire business began."

"There you go," he said, grinning at me. "He played you. But don't feel bad. He's an actor and you're, what, sixteen, seventeen?"

There you go, stroking my ego to make me feel big and impor-tant. You're smooth, like a snake.

Almost mumbling, I said, "I turn fifteen this month, but let me ask you—is there anything Forester had, other than Randolph Manor, that someone would want?"

"Nothing except Mrs. Forester. I'm sure you noticed she's quite attractive. I also happen to know the county coroner has a thing for her."

"Dr. Edwards?"

"Don't let his title fool you. He received a doctoral degree in philosophy from an online university. He lets people think he's a medical doctor. It works, too. He keeps getting elected county coroner."

"So he doesn't have any medical training?"

"Only what he's picked up on the job. That's why he works at the car dealership. He has to do something that actually pays the bills. He works in their accounting department. My niece works in the service department and she's told me a couple of times about how they've asked Edwards to stop leaving flowers in the front seat of Lucy's car. It's against company policy for anyone but the technicians to be in the vehicle while it's being serviced."

"Mrs. Forester said she had a friend who helped her with her blog. Do you think she meant Dr. Edwards?"

He sipped from a water glass and glanced around the dining room before turning his full attention back on me. "You like this, don't you? Asking all these questions." He dabbed his mouth with a napkin, then said, "I would imagine Edwards would be pretty handy with computers. If Lucy needed help and she asked Edwards, I'm sure he'd jump at the chance. But you didn't hear that from me. I don't want Lucy any madder at me than she already is."

"What do you think happened on your golf course, Mr. Hamilton?"

With a pained expression he said, "I wish I knew, I honestly do. Bottom line? I think Forester keeled over and somebody, Barlow maybe, dragged him onto number thirteen and drove a stake into him. He's the only one I can think of crazy enough to try a stunt like that. Fame and money, that's my guess. Barlow needs both."

I told him I appreciated his time and excused myself.

Hamilton had one theory on what happened to Forester's body. Maybe Barlow did have something to do with it, but I had another idea of how Forester's body ended up on the golf course: one that did not involve Barlow or Raintree or any vampire game.

Only thing left to do was test my theory against the television episodes and see if I was right.

CHAPTER TWELVE
DEAD WRONG

While walking under the breezeway connecting the main building to the Last Resort Shopping Market, I laid out several possible scenarios for how Barnabas Forester ended up dead.

One idea was that Barlow found Forester dead, probably from a heart attack, like Hamilton suggested, and dumped the body on the golf course. *We'll call that means. But why? Just for a few quotes in the media?* I pondered Barlow's motive and means against the risk. Was Barlow really so desperate to resurrect his acting career that he'd risk jail time by desecrating a body? Or maybe get himself arrested on murder charges? Besides, according to Barlow, he was out of town the night Forester died. But if not Barlow, then...

Perhaps Raintree. Maybe the bookstore owner panicked when he heard Forester was about to renege on the land deal. If Lieutenant McAlhany was right, the bookstore wasn't the success it appeared to be, and Raintree certainly didn't appear to be the type of person who could stand the public ridicule resulting from bankruptcy. He could die a thousand deaths from the lips of small-town gossips — he knew that better than anyone. His cultured persona struck me as contrived and prideful. Winding up as head of a nonprofit with even a small but stable salary would solve a lot of Raintree's problems, especially if the vampire slayer game wasn't doing well. But that would only happen if Forester's will left the land to the wildlife group. Or...

Maybe Lucy Forester found a chance to ditch her husband for good before he could drag her down in his spiraling depression. Her car had been at the crime scene and no one could vouch for her the night of "Barry's" death. Had she approached her husband about reconciling their differences so that he would put her in his will? Was that what she and Hamilton were discussing at her house? Or...

Had Victor Hamilton figured out a way to seize the Randolph estate in probate court? Could be if Forester's will became muddled, Hamilton and Lucy Forester might be able to combine their efforts and keep the property from going to Raintree's nonprofit. It wouldn't be the first time a businessman killed his rival in order to grab land. Or...

Dr. Edwards killed Forester because he had a crush on the dead man's wife. Or...

There really were such things as vampires, and Forester was one of several roaming the countryside of Transylvania. The business in the alley still haunted me. I still smelled the mugger's stale breath and felt his clammy hands on my throat. Of all the scenarios I rehearsed in my mind, that one seemed the most vivid and frightening.

☠

I found Meg chatting with a salesclerk at the checkout register of a gift shop. I caught her attention and pointed to my phone, then stepped outside to phone Dad.

"How's the story coming along, son?"

"Okay. I have lots of leads but I'm having trouble settling on one suspect. I've narrowed it down to five or six."

"Sounds like you still have some work to do."

"Yeah, but I think I'll get a better idea of who the killer is once I see the report."

"Report?"

"I'm running a search of our database to see if I can find episodes that match the circumstances surrounding this case. Sorry I didn't call earlier. How'd Wendy do last night?"

"Here, I'll let her tell you."

I leaned against the railing of a wooden walkway that overlooked a man-made lagoon. A circular fountain stood in the middle of the pond. Atop the foundation was a fat bronze sculpture of Cupid holding a water pitcher under his arm.

Clothing stores and quaint boutiques lined the walkway. Inside the large front window of a pastry shop, children camped on stools while a pastry chef decorated a three-tier cake. Someone was having a birthday. *Birthday—oh my gosh, I forgot mine's coming up. I haven't even told Mom and Dad what I want.*

Wendy's snarky comment yanked me back to the call.

"Have you reached a dead end yet?"

"Good one, sis, that's funny. How'd you do last night?"

"Fourth place."

"Hey, that's great. I mean, it's not first, but wow, fourth, that's awesome."

"What happened, did you fall on your head? You never say anything nice about my cheerleading."

"Sure I do."

"Yeah? When?"

I eased toward the doorway of the bakery and inhaled the sweet smell of fresh-baked brownies. "Just then."

"I meant before."

"Before what?"

"Before now, you goober."

One of the salesladies passed me a small, dark square on a toothpick. I wolfed it down and asked my sister, "How far away are you? It's getting sort of lonely not having anyone to pick on."

"We're stuck in traffic. You know Dad and his shortcuts. He thought driving *through* Atlanta would be shorter than taking the interstate."

I could hear Dad in the background yelling it *would* have been shorter if the stupid GPS hadn't sent him through the middle of the Georgia Tech campus. From down the walkway, I saw Meg exit the gift shop and come ambling toward me.

"So what're we looking at? Another five hours before you get here?"

I listened to Wendy ask Dad and then him yelling to her: "WE'LL BE THERE WHEN WE GET THERE!"

"Got it," I told her. "Maybe you can ring me back when you're on the other side of Atlanta. We should probably work out where we're going to meet." I motioned to the saleslady for another brownie sample and handed it to Meg. "Hey, Wendy?"

"Yeah?"

"All kidding aside, I really, really am happy for you. I know how hard you worked. Tell Dad no more shortcuts."

"Thanks, big brother. See ya when I see ya."

I snagged Meg another brownie sample and waved a Last Resort brochure at her.

"Did you know this is one of the top golfing resorts in the state?"

"I did not."

"Here, listen to this: 'Noted for its understated elegance and southern charm, the Last Resort has served as the backdrop for countless movies and hosted dinners for international dignitaries. Guests can relax in one of 212 rooms and themed suites, enjoy a drink by a massive fourteen-foot fireplace, or watch the sunset from a rocking chair overlooking the Great

Smokey Mountains. Last Resort boasts three dining facilities, an eighteen-hole golf course, a tennis and fitness center, an award-winning spa, and spacious convention facilities.'"

"Thinking of booking a room?"

"Just saying, Victor Hamilton and his partners have done pretty well for themselves. I can see why he would want to get his hands on the rest of the Randolph property. If he doubled the size of this place, he might have the largest golf resort in the Carolinas." I tucked the pamphlet in my back pocket and nodded toward the gift bag. "Can I see what you bought?"

Meg pulled out a snow globe. "It's for your aunt. She's been so nice, driving us around, helping you get in to see people. I thought she might like something as a souvenir of our 'great caper.'"

"Speaking of which, I think I've narrowed down our list of suspects to five, but I'm leaning toward one in particular."

"Really? Who? And don't tell me Dr. Edwards."

"Okay, I won't."

"You can't be serious. I already told you, he—"

"'Wouldn't hurt a fly,' 'is as pure as the driven snow,' 'a model citizen,' you pick the cliché. Probably helps old ladies cross the street, buys every kind of Girl Scout cookie there is, and volunteers at the soup kitchen on his days off."

"Stop being such a jerk—this is my boss we're talking about."

"Did you know he's not even a doctor?"

"Is too."

"Of medicine?"

"I, ah ... never thought to ask."

"Come on, I need to figure this out before it gets dark, and to do that I need your laptop."

We left the shopping area and returned to the resort's main lobby. Colorful oriental rugs covered marble floors; ornate chandeliers hung from dark wooden beams. Guests sat in rocking chairs on the patio and watched the sun setting behind the Blue Ridge Mountains. We dropped into comfy chairs and Meg got out her laptop. My goal was to see if I could find any connections between the circumstances surrounding Forester's death and a TV show that featured similar elements.

I opened the database report I'd run from our TV Crime Watchers website. The first listing was a summary of an episode from a television show called *'Til Death Do You Part*.

"Before I start reading, I want to make a prediction. I bet these results will reveal the killer in all these shows was a jilted lover."

Meg leaned from her chair and clamped down on my arm, squeezing it hard. "I don't know how many ways I can say this: Dr. Edwards did not kill anybody." Her tone got a little more desperate. "You have to trust me on this."

"Fine, whatever," I said, not convinced. "You take notes. Jot down character profiles and motives."

"Why can't I read and you take notes?"

"You have better penmanship. I want the lieutenant to be able to read this when we're done."

I moved the laptop into my lap. "This episode is called 'Skyfall.'"

A man sits in a leather chair with a book in his lap. Heavy drapery covers the window. A half-empty liquor bottle sits on a small table next to his chair. Glass empty. Suddenly a whispering voice calls to him. Man looks toward French doors leading onto a balcony. Nothing. He goes back to reading. Bedside lamp flickers, balcony door blows open. Man stands and walks outside. Wind blows through trees, a limb rakes the side of the house. We see him leaning over the railing and looking down at a candle moving mysteriously across the back lawn. In the door's reflection we see a translucent figure approaching from behind and...

Next morning: Scene opens with the show's main character, a quirky detective who constantly repeats what people say to him, standing beneath the balcony looking up. Local deputy working the case admits he's never handled a homicide before. Body lies facedown on bloodstained cement. Deputy announces the victim is a forty-three-year-old recluse suffering from depression. Separated from his wife. No children. Victim was fascinated with the occult and bought the house with hopes of turning it into his own private museum featuring paranormal artifacts. Deputy speculates the man probably committed suicide.

I continued reading aloud until I reached the summary paragraph and stopped.

Peering over at Meg, I asked, "Well, who are our suspects?"

"So far you've mentioned a deputy, a bookstore owner, the victim's wife, a handyman hired to make improvements, a professional rival, the real estate agent who handled the purchase of the home, and . . ." She turned over her page of notes. "That's it."

"Let's match that with what we know of Forester's situation. We'll call the deputy our Lieutenant McAlhany; obviously Raintree is the bookstore owner. Lucy Forester, the wife. I see the handyman hired to fix the home as our vampire expert, Barlow. Victor Hamilton is the professional rival."

"Sounds like you could have written this script."

"Except we also have Henry, the maintenance worker who found the body, and your boss."

"I told you, Dr. Edwards—"

"Wouldn't hurt a fly, I know. Let's see who the killer turns out to be." I silently read the rest of the synopsis. "Just as I thought: the real estate agent killed the husband."

"But why?"

"Fell in love with the victim's wife. Then when the couple began talking about reconciling, he got worried. He was afraid she might go back to the husband, so he pushed the poor guy from the balcony and made it look like the handyman had installed a faulty railing."

I straightened and glanced around the lobby. "What time was Aunt Vivian meeting you?"

"She didn't say exactly, but she told me she'd stop by the gift shop first. If I wasn't there, she'd look for me in here."

"In that case, I'll read a few more."

I reviewed an episode called "House of Horrors" from the television show *CBI Sacramento*. As before, Meg took notes of characters and motivations.

"Same M.O.," I said, finishing the summary. "Jilted lover kills fiancé."

"Still no sign of your aunt," Meg said. "She must be making up for all those Christmases your family never spent with her."

There were five episodes in all. I quickly went through the last three: "Mummy's Little Helper" from *Law and Murder*, "Danger at Dead Low Tide" from *Skull and Bones*, and "Hacker's Forward Slash" from *Our Man in Budapest*. Each episode centered on the purchase of a home, a pseudo-paranormal event, and a murder with a romantic interest who turned out to be the killer.

"None of this proves anything," Meg said. "You can't solve a crime from watching TV."

"It proves one thing. It proves your boss falling in love with Lucy Forester and killing her husband isn't that crazy of an idea. He's been buying her flowers, did you know that? I discovered that little piece of information from reading the card on the arrangement of daisies sitting in Mrs. Forester's painting studio. Here's another thing I learned: Hamilton has a niece who works at the dealership. She claims your boss was told to stop leaving things in Mrs. Forester's vehicle when it was in the shop. By the way, when I asked Mrs. Forester where she was that night, she claimed her car was in the shop all week. But the maintenance boy said he saw Lucy Forester's car in the employee parking lot the morning Forester's body was found."

"Maybe he only *thought* it was her car."

"Possibly. But I have another idea about what happened. I think Edwards didn't want to be seen driving his car to and from the crime scene so he borrowed Mrs. Forester's."

"But wouldn't that implicate her in the murder?"

"Yes, but it would be easy enough to check and find out she couldn't have driven the car to the resort because it was in the shop and she couldn't get it out of the dealership lot. Look, I'm not saying it happened exactly that way; I'm just saying I think her car was at the crime scene and the only person who had access to it was your boss. Maybe the maintenance boy didn't see the car there. Maybe he was confused. But don't forget, your boss is one of the few people who could have implanted fangs and added bite marks. I know he's not a physician, but he probably has some medical skills, right?"

"Ah ... yes, but—"

"My guess is, after your boss found out I was looking into the case, he panicked and moved the body before I could prove he murdered Forester."

Meg rolled her eyes at me. "You got all this out of five stupid television shows? Unbelievable."

"It's not all that hard, Meg. People watch TV, get an idea, and act on it. It's called a copycat crime."

She released my arm and sat back in her chair. "You can't prove any of this."

I could tell she wasn't buying it. I just sighed and said, "I don't have to *prove* anything. I'll let Lieutenant McAlhany build the case against your boss. My job is to flush the killer out into the open and write the story based on the facts as I know them."

"You're not sending your article from my laptop, I'll tell you that. Not if you insist on accusing Dr. Edwards of murder."

"Fine. I'm sure the hotel has a media center where I can borrow a computer."

"Don't, please," she pleaded. "I'm begging you."

"Why? What's the big deal? If he's a killer, wouldn't you want him locked up?"

She got this hopeless expression on her face, one that made me feel bad for doubting her. My gut told me she honestly believed her boss was innocent, but how could she be so sure?

"Hey, Meg, I'm sorry. I'm not trying to be mean or anything. I'm just looking at the evidence, but if you know something, I need to know it. What aren't you telling me?"

"Dr. Edwards is dating my mom, okay? That's how I know he could not possibly be involved with Mrs. Forester."

"Okay, that's some news I could have used earlier."

"That night Forester died? Dr. Edwards was at our house. *All night.* That's why I'm sure he didn't kill anyone."

The *woop-woop* of an ambulance interrupted me before I could suggest that Edwards slipped out of Meg's house without anybody knowing. Seconds later two paramedics rushed through the front door and went charging across the lobby and down the hallway toward the shopping area. Guests and hotel staff stood gawking. A woman in a tennis outfit cornered a bellhop and demanded to know what was going on.

"Someone collapsed outside the gift shop. It might have been a heart attack."

I found myself running after the paramedics without any recollection of leaving my chair. Kids spilled out of the bakery shop, blocking my path. A forest of heads and shoulders made it impossible to see down the walkway. I lowered my shoulder and shoved my way toward the front of the crowd.

Aunt Vivian lay on her back, the contents of her purse spilled onto the walkway. Her face was sallow, mouth slack. Eyes unfocused.

Talking to each other in low voices, the medics slid Aunt Vivian onto a stretcher, uncoiled the gurney's legs and rolled her away. I followed behind, watching as EMTs tossed medical equipment bags into the back of the ambulance. The last time I'd felt that stunned was when I'd found our dog on the side of the highway.

They put Aunt Vivian into the truck, and one of them settled into a jump seat beside her. Standing at the rear of the ambulance, I blinked away tears as the paramedic slammed the door shut and got behind the wheel.

"She'll be okay," a security guard said to me.

I wiped my eyes with the back of my wrist. "You don't know that."

"She'll be okay," he repeated.

But I wasn't so sure. Aunt Vivian definitely didn't *look* okay. Meg suddenly appeared by my side carrying Aunt Vivian's purse and shopping bags.

"Get my laptop," she said to me.

"What?"

"I'm bringing your aunt's car around. I'll drive you to Asheville General."

"But you don't have your license."

"My laptop! Hurry!"

CHAPTER THIRTEEN
CRYPTIC MESSAGES

I trotted back into the lobby carrying a leaden feeling of hopelessness. *Aunt Vivian, in an ambulance, just like she'd feared.* "About the only exciting thing that happens at 'the home' is when an ambulance comes to cart one of us away," she'd told me in the car before we went inside the morgue. "God help me, Nick, I don't want to go out that way. Let me tag along with you, please? I want to have some fun."

Some fun.

The crowd of rubberneckers began to drift away. Bellhops loaded bags onto luggage carts; front desk clerks swiped credit cards as guests checked in. From the bar came the sound of ice cubes clanking into sturdy drinking glasses. I couldn't get the sight of Aunt Vivian out of my mind. *Dad's right. Family is everything.*

I had thought he was doing me a favor by letting me travel to Transylvania alone, and he was, but the real gift was Aunt Vivian. She was by far the best part of the trip. I had pictured Dad's aunt as a cranky, demanding old woman who was annoyed at having to babysit me, but she'd been the exact opposite. I could tell all our running around had left her tired, but she hadn't complained. Just the opposite — she acted like I should be doing *more* to catch the killer. Aunt Vivian had become the sweet grandmother I'd never had, the one they make movies about where the actress playing the part gets an Oscar. That's what Aunt Vivian was — a Golden Globe – winning aunt.

I reached the area where we'd been sitting but stopped well short of the chairs. Meg's laptop was open, lid up, with a line of text on the screen. I whirled around but didn't see anyone darting away. I went over and peered down at the screen. Instantly my pulse began to race.

Congratulations, Nicholas, you ALMOST solved the case.

I jerked my head around again, expecting to find someone watching me, but saw no one. More text crawled across the page.

Sit, we need to talk.

I remained hunched over the laptop, my palms damp with sweat.

I said SIT!

Dropping into the chair, I angled the laptop so only I could read the mysterious message.

Too bad about your aunt. She seems like such a nice person. It would be a shame if something happened to her ... or that sweet girl, Meg, who you like so much. ☹

The frowning face made my stomach flip. I whipped my head around. No sign of Meg with Aunt Vivian's Cadillac.

Forester was murdered, that much you guessed correctly, but not with a wooden stake. The medical examiner found enough viable muscle tissue to rule his death a heart attack, so you might say Forester died of a broken heart. That's a little joke, Nicholas. I would expect at least a smile.

No way could I smile; my heart was racing too fast.

Lieutenant McAlhany can confirm the medical examiner's findings. McAlhany received the autopsy report this evening, I made certain of it. In fact, I personally delivered Forester's body to the Buncomb County medical examiner. I did not want you or the lieutenant drawing the wrong conclusions about this case. A jilted lover, indeed. How foolish you were to think Dr. Edwards could possibly kill someone. Or Barlow, Hamilton, or Forester's wife. And of course now he cannot kill anyone. He's dead too.

I checked over my shoulder, desperately hoping to see Aunt Vivian's car pulling up.

Stop wasting time, Nicholas. Soon the dark shadows of dusk will fall upon the mountain and you know what that means. Now I'm afraid it is too late. Bad things must happen and you are to blame.

I scooted to the edge of the chair and tried to tamp down the feeling of panic building inside me.

Forester was not a vampire, but you knew this already. I added the fangs and bite marks. Nice touch, don't you think? By the way, I left a comment for your editor on that foolish ghoul website explaining that you would not be filing the final draft of your story. We had a lovely chat; it's all there in the replies, if you care to look. He sounded disappointed to learn he would be losing such an eager young reporter, but I assured him your untimely "termination" could not be avoided.

I took a final quick peek back at the drop-off area, hoping to see Aunt Vivian's Cadillac. *Meg, where are you? This isn't funny.*

You think you're so smart, Nicholas Caden. You with your television show detecting. Can you guess what comes next? No? Do I have to draw you a map? Very well. I left one in the side pocket of your backpack.

I looked down and I saw my backpack and Barlow's medical bag wedged between the chairs.

Yes, I retrieved your things for you. I knew you would not be returning to your room. Not ... ever.

Now then, I "suspect" you have already guessed I am waiting for you. The map will lead you there. But just so you are not surprised when you arrive, here is a little riddle: Monsters like us "reign" forever. We "book" our rooms in caskets and caves and roam the countryside in both day and night, just like the wolf. You will find your aunt's car parked under the "tree" at the graveyard.

"Suspect ... book ... reign ... tree." *Raintree? He's the killer?*

Come alone, Nicholas. For Meg's sake, come alone.

CHAPTER FOURTEEN
DUSK TO DAWN

I found Aunt Vivian's car parked in the middle of a weedy field near a row of grave markers. I had not told the resort's shuttle driver the real reason I needed to get off the shuttle halfway down the mountain, only that I wanted to walk the hiking trail back up to the resort.

Standing by the road, I studied the instructions left to me in my backpack: *Place your backpack and the medical bag on the front passenger seat and put your phone in the cup holder. I will know if you do not.*

I did as ordered and slammed the car door shut. *No tools and no way to call for help. Great.* The route had been highlighted in yellow. My journey began with a large X next to the gnarled oak overlooking an abandoned graveyard. I knew I was walking into a trap, but what choice did I have? Aunt Vivian's car parked in the field proved Raintree was deadly serious about me finding him alone.

A buzzard came winging in low and circled the giant oak before settling on a branch. Turkey vultures are scavengers. They feed almost exclusively on the carcasses of animals and rodents and have laser-sharp eyes. But it's their keen sense of smell that draws them to roadside kills and wooded hills with freshly dug graves.

I choked down the bile rising in my throat. If I was going to catch the killer and save Meg, I needed to become as calm as Raintree.

I followed a serpentine path across matted grass toward the tree line. Mountain shadows had turned green pines purplish-blue. Crickets chirped, gnats buzzed. Several yards into the woods I found the old logging road mentioned on the map. The road was little more than a foot trail. Dusk settled over the forest; the air grew cool. With each step I felt smaller and weaker. I had to keep reminding myself that Meg was ahead of me, waiting for me to save her. It took every ounce of courage to keep from running back to the car and calling the lieutenant.

Or Dad.

I picked up the pace, walking briskly up the darkened path. I'd been walking maybe fifteen minutes when I came to a mossy area guarded by towering spruces and pines. Though an edge of light sky remained in the western sky, the moon was already up and growing brighter as the sun set behind the mountains. Ferns sprouted from dead tree stumps, and a wispy haze cloaked the ground. I kept telling myself it would be okay, that I'd find Meg and all of it would turn out to be one big hoax, that someone—maybe her—was yanking my chain. She had insisted Edwards wasn't the killer. Maybe this was her way of getting back at me for thinking her boss was the killer.

All I could picture, though, was Meg getting into Aunt Vivian's Cadillac and a cold hand stifling her screams.

The breeze bending the treetops carried with it the sour odor of rot and decay. Twilight is a time of endings. End of work, end of day, end of sunlight and the freedom it brings.

The cooing of the wind fell away, leaving only the sound of my footsteps crunching dried underbrush. I reached the spillway we'd crossed the night before and paused. Behind me I heard snapping and crunching, like something prowling about. I pivoted and strained to see through the dark gray mist. My pulse quickened. I remembered how the wolf dog had appeared out of the fog and moved with phantom speed as it chased the carriage. *Is there one or more? A pack, maybe?*

My heart pounded against the walls of my chest. I began a slow, measured jog up the trail, trotting farther into the woods until only the moon's silver light penetrated the mist. The moon's glow gave the forest an eerie green, phosphorescent tint. Again, leaves rustled behind me; once more I stopped and looked. Now I heard the heavy pounding of something barreling through the forest, snapping limbs and crushing leaves underfoot.

I raced toward the sound of rushing water, knowing if I could reach Skull Creek I'd find sanctuary in the catacomb I'd used to escape the manor. If the map was accurate, it wasn't far ahead.

Out of the corner of my eye I saw movement, looked left, and in the moonlight caught a glimpse of the wolf dog darting through the mist. Its shaggy fur glistened silver in the damp air. I darted behind a pine and stood perfectly still. The tree provided no comfort, none at all. The wolf dog went past the trees in a brisk, bouncy trot, the way an animal will when it's on a scent and ready to sprint in for the kill.

Past me and toward the creek it trotted. Then I saw its prey. A stag buck stood on the opposite bank. Its rack was ten points at least. The deer lowered its head to graze by the water's edge, then looked up quickly, presenting a long, meaty brown throat. For several long seconds the stag stood frozen in the silver moonlight.

I slipped from behind the tree and circled down toward the creek, moving away while being careful not to make a sound. I reached the creek a good ways downstream and paused, looking for smooth stones I could step on to cross. The stag bent its neck and looked at me. Large mule ears angled toward me.

The wolf dog sprang with a deathly silence. Its claws clamped onto the deer's haunch and deadly fangs sank into the stag's throat. A ragged, pulsating gash opened that sent blood spewing into the creek. Under the weight of the wolf dog, the stag's front legs buckled, and both fell splashing into the gurgling water now brown with blood. For several horrifying seconds I stood stunned, too afraid to move as the deer fought to kick free, but with fierce bites the wolf dog ripped away large chunks of meat with a savageness that sickened me.

At last I tore my gaze away and went splashing across the creek and up the other side. Behind me, I heard gnarling and snapping and a terrible sound out of the stag's wheezing cries for help. Running became the only thing that mattered. I darted around trees and up the sloping forest floor with small plants slapping at my legs. In the moonlight I saw a clearing hollowed out in the woods. As I drew closer I realized it was a stone crypt, one built into the side of the hill. Vines choked its rusty bars. Gargoyle sculptures looked down from atop two massive columns supporting the overhang covering a short stoop. A half-opened gate anchored the center of an iron fence running around the stoop.

The wolf dog's victory howl echoed through the forest and was followed instantly by the thunder of paws approaching. I chanced a single backward glance — just one — and saw the beast charging after me, its fur sodden by the stag's blood, eyes yellow and glowing in the moon's light. I hit the metal bars with my shoulder and knocked the gate open, fell inside, and slammed the gate shut with my foot.

Before I could sit up and slide the latch into place, the wolf dog erupted from the forest, charged across the small meadow of damp grass, and lunged at the gate. Its front paws hit with such force that the impact sent me skidding backward across slate tiles. I thrust my feet forward, closing the gate on the animal's head. With bloody fangs inches from my face, I kicked the bars a final time and forced the wolf dog back, then reached up and shoved the latch into place. The beast responded by slamming into the gate again, but the latch held.

I scooted all the way across the tiles until my back rested against the front door's heavy wood paneling. Terrified by the wolf dog's rabid snapping and growling and hyped up on adrenaline, I could not make my hands stop shaking. Finally I reached over my head, turned the door's knob, and fell back inside. Still on my back, I wormed my way in and slammed the door shut. I lay on the cold slate tiles in the darkness and listened, my heart hammering in my chest.

The crypt smelled like mildew, a tangy odor of rodents, and damp rot. A needle of moonlight came through the crack in the door and provided some light, but not enough to get a good idea of the size of the room. The rustle of cloth approached from somewhere behind me. I sensed a heavy shadow standing over me. A voice, no, a whisper, blew into my ear.

"So good of you to join me, Nicholas. I know you are *dying* to close this case, so let's begin."

CHAPTER FIFTEEN
THE SLEEP OF DEATH

A match raked against the slate flooring. Its flame lit a slender white candle. For a half second I could almost make out the face of the individual holding the wrought-iron candleholder, the silhouette of chin, cheek, and forehead. It might have been male, but I couldn't be sure.

I pushed myself onto my elbows. "Where is Meg?" I asked, trying to sound braver than I felt.

"At the hospital, I would imagine. I put her in the ambulance with the driver and told them we would be right behind them in your aunt's car."

I sat up and watched a bone-white hand place the candleholder atop a stone casket. Before I could get a clear look at the face, the silky black cape slipped back into shadows. There were two rows of caskets, each one elevated above dusty flagstone tiles by stone blocks. Outside at the gate the wolf dog's snarling ceased, leaving only the moaning of limbs creaking as a breeze pushed through the forest.

"Did you know Elizabeth Bathory is probably the most prolific female serial killer of all time?"

I could not be sure if the voice was Raintree's or not. Not that it mattered; whoever it was had me trapped.

"While her husband was on the front lines, she murdered six hundred people, maybe more. Many of them young women. Bathory believed that by bathing in the blood of young girls she could obtain immortality. How about you? Do you believe a person can gain eternal life through the blood of another?"

"I, ah ... haven't really thought about it."

"You lie." The phantom figure strolled about the room as though taking inventory of the caskets, always remaining just beyond the edge of light.

"The question of life after death through the consumption of blood has consumed you since you arrived. Why else would you be here? Was this not why you jumped at the chance to investigate Forester's death? Because you secretly wondered if the rumors were true: that there are such things as vampires and, if there are, there might also be the chance for immortal life?"

"Hadn't really thought about any of it." I stood and looked for an opportunity to bolt. "Was just looking to write a story.

That's what I do. As long as my readers like my article, it doesn't much matter to me if there's life after death."

"Please step away from the door. I would so hate for Moses to tear out your throat before we finished our chat."

A bitter taste filled my mouth. It was the same dry-mouth sensation I feel every time one of my teachers announces a pop quiz. It's the rush of adrenaline followed by a sense of failure.

I released my grip on the brass knob and stepped away from the door. "Who are you? What do you want?"

"Did you know if the body remains faceup after the heart stops pumping, the vessels in the back of the legs become clogged with blood? Without oxygen, anaerobic fermentation sets in. This produces lactic acid, which in turn causes rigor mortis. Should the body remain undiscovered and untouched for several hours, insects begin arriving. Flies lay eggs in the nose, mouth, and ears. Maggots hatch and begin eating the decomposing flesh."

"Why are you telling me this?"

"I thought these sorts of things fascinated you. Is that not why you watch all those murder investigation shows? To study about death and killing?"

In the flame's faint glow I saw the shadowy figure rub a pale hand over a casket. The voice was male, that I knew. But not Raintree's. Or Barlow's.

"The digestion of the body's cells releases gases, giving the corpse that putrid smell. After four days, the skin begins to look like cottage cheese. Fluids leak out, attracting more insects. But of course you know all this, or should. Is that not why you insisted on seeing Forester's body? To satisfy your curiosity?"

Instantly I identified the voice. "Dr. Edwards?" I watched the shadowy shape turn toward me. "But I thought you were ..."

"Dead? Hardly." Edwards strolled between the rows of caskets and stopped next to the candle. "I admit when you arrived this morning asking to see Forester's body, it caught me off guard. It hadn't occurred to me an outsider might be interested in the case. I suppose Raintree is to thank for that miscalculation. I should have guessed he might try to use Forester's death as a media event for his obtuse vampire slayer game. Is he the one who tipped you off to Forester's death?"

"I ... we traced the IP address of the person who posted the tip. It came from Transylvania."

"Idiot man, always the media hound."

"So I was right about you. You did kill Forester."

"Why, but of course. Just as I will kill you. Please do not keep edging toward the door."

"But why? If you really are in love with his wife, why not wait for the divorce to go through?"

"Do you really think a woman of Lucy's tastes finds me interesting? To her I am a friendly neighbor, the fix-it buddy who stops by to help her when she cannot remember how to open a Web browser. Forester knew of my interest in his wife. He warned me to stop pursuing her. Fool. Who does he think he is telling me who I can and cannot love?"

"But you're dating Meg's mom."

"Merely a convenient diversion until I can win Lucy's heart. And I will. In time she will find me the stable, caring man Forester never could be."

I had to keep him talking, keep him engaged. Last thing I could do was let him see my disappointment at being tricked.

As calmly as I could I said, "Whatever you're planning, it won't work. As soon as Meg figures out I'm not behind her in Aunt Vivian's car, she'll call me."

"I doubt that very much. I doubt anyone will find you for a very long time. And when they do, this business with Forester will be of no consequence to anyone. As soon as I am able, I plan to suggest to Lucy that she move. This dreary place is really too small for a woman of her talents. But that is none of your concern. Now, walk slowly toward that coffin. Yes, that one there. Good."

"You're more talkative than you were this morning."

"Let's say I'm chatty because I know there is nothing I say that will . . . come back to haunt me. That one right there. Yes, that's it. Open it."

I eyed the coffin by my elbow. It was diamond-shaped like those pine boxes you see in old westerns, the kind with more room at the head and shoulders than legs and feet.

"What now?"

"Isn't it obvious? You become the lead character of a *Cool Ghoul* article: a truly dead lead that gets buried at the bottom of the page."

I couldn't let him see how scared I was, though honestly I wasn't sure how I could hide it. My legs shook with the force of an earthquake.

"Did you send Forester's body to the medical examiner, or was that a hoax too?"

"What do you think? You are the expert."

Keep him talking, Caden, keep him talking. "I think you buried the body someplace and everything you wrote on Meg's laptop, you made up."

"You are correct. Right outside as a matter of fact. You probably did not notice the fresh grave because Moses was chasing you. No one will think to look behind the hedge of rhododendrons. Vultures, perhaps, but that is all."

I looked at him with disbelief. "*You* dug a grave?"

I could not imagine Edwards with his limp, sweaty hands and flabby paunch could do something that strenuous.

"With a backhoe on an ATV. What, you thought I walked here?"

"Won't someone wonder when Forester's body doesn't come back from the medical examiner?"

"I have an urn full of ashes. It was Forester's wish to be cremated. Lucy will not question it. The lieutenant is satisfied with the autopsy report. Raintree will use news of the death of the 'Dark Coven Master' as a way to boost book sales in his store, I'm sure of it. Barlow gets quoted in your latest and final article. His reputation may take a hit once the press learns he has been charged with mutilating a body, but perhaps even that will help. Who is to say? Right now Lucy is in shock, though she doesn't know it. Her pending divorce and Forester's death have left her emotionally confused. Once I prove myself to be the steady rock she can count on, the shoulder to cry on, she will see me in a new light."

"Seriously? You killed Forester just to steal his wife?"

"Oh, please. You think I'm the first? This tale is as old as David and Bathsheba."

"David and Bath what?"

"What *are* they teaching kids in Sunday school these days?"

"We don't go to church. Mom and Dad don't believe in it."

"Pity. A solid moral foundation is the backbone of civilized people."

I wanted to reply, "Yeah, well, it didn't do much good for you," but I didn't. Instead I said, "Walk it back for me, the timeline of the murder."

"I do not see where that can hurt. You will not be alive to tell anyone. Let's see, I snuck into the manor the evening before. I came by way of the catacombs. I think we both know what I mean by that. I found Forester asleep in that dreadful casket. I had made it a point over the past few months to befriend Moses, so we are almost best friends now. I gave him a tough rib eye, one I purchased on sale. While he ate I anesthetized Forester, first with chloroform, and followed that with a second cocktail of drugs. Once he was unconscious I drained his blood. This took the better part of an hour."

"How did you carry it out?"

"The blood? Three half-gallon jugs. To keep Moses happy I gave him a second piece of beef. Removing the body proved more difficult. Medical stretchers do not roll well through catacombs, but I managed. I had parked Lucy's car on the carriage road that runs between the manor and guesthouse. I drove to the resort, carefully placed Forester on the putting green, and returned to the dealership. I picked up my car and snuck back into Meg's house and began preparing breakfast."

"Why go to all that trouble of making Forester look like a vampire?"

"People were bound to wonder what became of the man. He dressed the part, anyway. All I had to do was add the fangs and drive that stake through his heart. Eventually I would become a suspect, maybe even the main suspect. Hamilton's niece and others would see to that. By making his death a freakish event, I created confusion. I knew if anyone looked hard enough, they would learn Raintree and Barlow were running a vampire game out of the manor. Most likely the focus of the investigation would turn to the list of recent players, the idea being maybe one of them killed Forester by mistake."

"So Raintree wasn't involved?"

"Not in the least. Nor was Barlow. All were mere props in my charade. Keeping Forester's blood was a mistake, but I wanted to run some tests to see if he had any diseases he might have passed on to Lucy. Then you arrived asking questions and I had to dispose of it.

"So you're the one who made the morgue look as if it had been vandalized?"

"Needed a diversion to keep you and Meg from suspecting me. Now that the lieutenant has the autopsy report proving Forester died of a heart attack, I can go back to leading my normal, boring life."

"Which is not so boring after all," I said.

"No, it is not."

"If you were worried about me finding out that you killed Forester, why not kill me in the alley? Why go to all this trouble?" I said, motioning toward the caskets.

"Alley? I'm not sure I know what you mean."

"This afternoon when you mugged me."

"I assure you I have no idea what you are talking about. I planted the remote access software on Meg's computer so I could track you two and keep informed of your progress. I consider that a stroke of pure genius. But I am not a violent man, at least not in that way."

Well, if it wasn't you, then who ... I shelved that question for later. He'd fooled me once; maybe he was doing it again. "What about Meg? She knows I suspected you."

His gaze drifted toward the coffin beside me. "Enough talking." He stepped closer, lifted the candle, and nodded at the coffin. "Open it."

I studied the simple black coffin with its rope handles and pine box smell.

"Please, I have another pressing engagement I need to keep."

He saw me hesitating and added, "Do not force me to bring Moses in here. He would leave things in such a bloody mess."

I could not believe I'd been right about Edwards. If only Aunt Vivian hadn't ... I forced my fingers under the edge of the lid. They felt like eight stubby lead crowbars prying under a slab of cement. I lifted a quarter inch, then a foot, then all the way.

Meg lay with hands folded across her chest and wrists bound with Aunt Vivian's knitting yarn. Her eyes were closed, silver tape across her mouth. In the candlelight her cheeks appeared porcelain smooth and drained of color. Her dark hair rested on her shoulders like the tail of a sleeping snake.

I felt a sudden sense of shock and horror. I pivoted quickly and hissed, "You told me she was on her way to the hospital."

"I lied."

"But why?"

"Loose ends. You never should have involved my assistant. Now I have no choice but to dispose of her too."

I turned back toward her. I wanted to touch her one last time, so I eased closer and squeezed her hand. To my surprise, it felt warm. I leaned over and pressed my lips to her ear and said softly, "Meg? Hey, Meg, it's me, Nick."

Eyelids lifted like a creaky garage door and stopped halfway up. Unfocused brown eyes rolled my direction and found my face. Soft dimpled cheeks crinkled under the tape as she forced a weak smile of recognition.

"Sorry I got you into this," I said, my voice breaking. "You were right. It's all my fault."

Her eyes softened just enough to let me know she got the joke. Then, just as suddenly, they grew wide with alarm. I hadn't noticed the candlelight moving closer, or Edwards's shadow falling over us. He clamped his hand over my mouth and pressed a rag firmly against my nose. With my sudden gasp, I breathed in the vapors wafting from the cloth. The room became a whirling fun ride at an amusement park, spinning and dipping and causing a roaring noise in my ears. I made a fumbling grab for Edwards's cloak and fell heavily, landing on the slate floor. In the half second before my world went dark, I heard Meg's muffled shriek.

Then I heard nothing at all.

CHAPTER SIXTEEN
SIX FEET UNDER

Claustrophobia is the fear of being confined in a small space without any hope of escape. A coffin qualifies. So does a grave. I came to the terrifying conclusion I'd been buried alive. In Meg's coffin. The smell of her lingered.

Six feet underground there is no light, none at all. Had the coffin rested on the ground or even on the sturdy stone casket supports inside the crypt, I would have detected a hint of moonlight. The sour smell of damp earth and the solid thump of my knuckles rapping the board above me led me to believe I'd been firmly planted.

I opened my eyes fully and yawned. Chloroform is a colorless, sweet-smelling, dense liquid commonly used as a solvent in labs. It's old school and cliché, but effective. And too much inhaled too quickly will kill someone. But I guessed Edwards knew the right amount to administer.

The vapors left me groggy and with a screaming headache. I wanted to go back to sleep, dream, and worry about escaping the coffin tomorrow. Or the next day. Or never.

At the most, a person can live four hours in a sealed casket—and that's if you work really hard to slow your breathing. I wasn't hyperventilating, not yet. But the longer I lay on my back thinking about where I was, how I got there, and what was probably happening to Meg, the more panic seemed to be the right option. I struggled to keep calm. I told myself I would get out, that help would come. I reminded myself that Dad and Mom were on their way, that they would find Aunt Vivian at the hospital but not me, and call the police. Maybe they were already searching for me.

But I also knew help might *not* arrive. Not for a very long time. If I hadn't noticed the grave in the clearing, would the lieutenant? Would anyone, ever?

The yawning subsided. I felt sweat trickling down my neck. Not from warmth but from anxiousness. My senses of smell, touch, and hearing slowly returned. The fog behind my eyes lifted. I pressed my knees against the lid and pushed. I shoved until my jaws ached and I thought my head would explode. The lid did not flex, not a bit.

Think, Caden, don't be stupid. You can't waste energy and air being stupid.

I remembered the rope handles I'd seen as I stared into Meg's coffin. I pivoted my hands until my palms faced outward. I groped in the darkness, feeling my way along the sides as far as the cramped space would allow. When my fingers found the rope, it felt like my very own lifeline. I gripped the cords, one in each hand, and pulled. There wasn't much slack in the ropes, but it was enough to give me hope.

Each rope was snaked through six holes: inside, out, back inside, out, and so on. I had hold of the middle section. There was just enough space to get my fingers between the rope and wooden sides.

Most boys my age don't wear belts. I don't know what belt manufacturers are going to do when Dad's generation dies off. Go out of business, I guess. But Mom, thank goodness, insists I wear a belt in public. I unbuckled and looped the belt over the left rope handle and buckled it, making it like a link in a chain. The belt reached halfway across the coffin and rested on my stomach. It took a lot longer to wiggle out of my tee, but I finally peeled it over my head. I rolled my shirt as tightly as I could and fed it through the rope hole on the right side of the coffin and secured it to the belt-link with a granny knot. Two links joined in the middle. Now all I needed was some type of lever.

A fat stick would be nice, or a wooden stake. Edwards had left me with nothing but a small vacuum of air, and that I gulped too fast.

The perfect tool is the one that gets the job done. Shucking my sneaker took a lot of effort. Hooking my leg, I scooted the shoe toward my left hand. The sneaker wasn't much of a lever, but it was all I had. I stuck the shoe end between the two strands of the belt and began winding it like a rubber band. No sweat. Even in total darkness I found it easy to twist the belt-rope—at first. But when it became so tight I couldn't take another turn, I paused to rethink my strategy. Holding the belt-rope in my left hand, I checked the sides. The coffin was definitely starting to bow in. Problem was, the sneaker didn't have any rigidity. I needed some way to keep the shoe stiff, but how? When nothing came to mind, I clamped both hands on the ball of the shoe and cranked as though turning a soft, pliable bar.

Wood splintering sounded encouraging. I cranked some more. A final turn and that was it; I couldn't twist it any more. I lifted my knee and wedged it against the shoe to hold it in place, braced my shoulder and head against the top end of the coffin, and pushed. Suddenly it was like the world collapsed on me. The sides cracked and broke and the lid shifted and fell. Dirt filled the space where the sides collapsed. I gave the belt another hard shove with my knee and more wood splintered, pulling the sides inward.

The sneaker slapped my stomach sharply as the belt unwound. Using my right hand I began shoveling dirt into the coffin, pulling it in, pushing it down, packing it with my feet. I scooped dirt and dumped it between my legs. When I had enough space to move my left elbow, I pressed my palm against the ragged edge of broken wood and pushed. More of the side broke away. I kept shoveling and got my feet into the action, pushing the dirt to the bottom of the coffin. The lid dipped toward one side. A seam opened on the other side. More dirt silted in.

I pawed at the dirt, pulling it in, shoveling it down. The work was messy and slow and tiring. I had to keep stopping to give my left arm a break. After what seemed like hours I was finally able to shove my head through the gap I'd created between the lid and crater in the earth. More digging, more grunting. I wiggled my shoulders out and sat up, ingesting a mouthful of dirt. Blindly I fumbled around for my shirt, found it, and pulled the fabric over my head, making a mask so I could breath without eating dirt.

I had no idea how deep the grave was. If Edwards went the full six feet, I could be digging for hours. Six feet is the depth at which odors cannot escape. At six feet, animals can't smell the rotting corpse and dig it up. Edwards struck me as a very thorough man.

The trick was to keep digging upward while at the same time packing the dirt down with my hands and elbows. The more I clawed my way out, the easier it became. Once I managed to get onto my knees, the digging went faster. I was a buried miner burrowing his way to life. Fatigue and dizziness from lack of oxygen became my biggest worry. I got into a rhythm and slowed my breathing to a slow panting.

I was still in a half crouch with my arms stretched over my head when my fingers poked through the surface. I can only imagine how it must have looked from up top — two darkened hands emerging from a grave, fingers flexing and reaching upward like night crawlers coming alive.

Once I was all the way out, I lay back on dirty wet grass and stared up at the moon. Its fullness shone down with such brilliance that I wanted to reach up and hug it.

I took one deep breath after another of clean, fresh air. I lay on the ground and listened for the wolf dog. When I heard nothing, I crawled to my feet and crept across the clearing, slipped past the iron gate, and peeked into the crypt. Only one coffin was missing. *That means he is on the move, taking Meg ... where? The morgue, maybe?*

I washed my face and hands in the creek. The stag lay by the water's edge, its mutilated carcass a brown lump in the moon's glow. Up the trail I crept, keeping my ears peeled for the wolf dog. When I reached the clearing, I saw that Aunt Vivian's car was gone.

I smiled.

Not because I was too late — but because Edwards had become careless.

I jogged back toward the highway and staggered up the road, waving my arms at oncoming traffic. I must have looked hideous with my clothes soiled by dirt and my face muddy. Headlights bore down on me. The approaching car swung out to pass me. I stepped in its path. Tires skidded, horn blared. I backpedaled just enough to keep the front grill from slamming into me. The driver's door flew open and before the man could finish cursing at me, I yelled back, "There's been a murder and kidnapping. I need to use your phone!"

☠

"Pearl-colored Cadillac, registered to Vivian Caden Carroll. That's right, Carroll, with two Ls." I listened as the operator repeated the owner information back to me. I said, "You have her living in Asheville, right? Okay, good, I'm going to give the phone to this police officer now."

I passed the phone to Lieutenant McAlhany. He listened, made a few notes in a spiral notepad, and hung up. "You caught a break with that GPS tracker in your aunt's car."

"I was due. Did the operator say where it is?" I asked.

McAlhany jerked his head down the highway. "Halfway between here and Asheville. Said the vehicle is stationary right now. You want to ride with me?"

"Please."

I gave the borrowed phone back to the driver and hurried around to the passenger's side of the squad car. I exhaled deeply, trying not to think of the worst-case scenario. *Please let her be alive, oh God, please.*

CHAPTER SEVENTEEN
DEAD END

Black is not my color. Black is the color of death and decay. Lately I've come to hate its suffocating darkness. Being buried alive will do that.

The three-piece suit fit perfectly. Dad said it made me look older. I felt ancient. I felt a thousand years old. I felt like a failure. If I had been thinking clearly in the lobby of the resort, I would have known there was no way Raintree was the person typing on Meg's laptop—that it had to be Edwards, and if it was, the smart move would have been to call the lieutenant. But I'd wanted to play the cowboy, ride in like the hero, and save the girl. *Stupid. Stupid, stupid, stupid.*

"You doing okay, son?"

I looked up from staring blankly at the blades of soft green grass poking up between my shoes.

"Sure, Dad. I'm fine."

The wooden slat of the folding chair bit my back. The stifling heat of the noon sun caused my white shirt to stick to my back. Ninety degrees in the Great Smoky Mountains and it felt like Arizona in August. No breeze at all, only the whining of insects vectoring in. I slapped the back of my neck.

Wendy leaned over and whispered, "It's okay if you want to cry. I won't tell."

"Shut up."

"It helps."

She passed me a tissue; I slapped her hand away.

"Would you two stop?" said Mom. "The service is about to start."

I followed her gaze and watched pallbearers approach the rear of the hearse. Six somber-faced sentinels, two of the boys not much older than me.

We stood. The men carefully lifted the chocolate-brown casket and walked it toward the grave site. Brown like the color of Meg's eyes. Rich and shiny and draped in a spray of flowers. The procession entered the tent and placed the casket onto its stand above the grave. I went back to staring at my feet. My new dress shoes cut across the tops of my toes; the narrow backs angled too sharply. I could tell I was going to end up with blisters. I didn't care. *Too proud to call for help. Too sure*

I'd guessed right about the killer. So sure, in fact, Edwards had used my arrogance against me. And Meg.

I hate funerals. All this talk about loved ones going off to be in a better place. It's nonsense. No one can prove what happens to us after we die. It's just talk. They should pass a law that says you can't promise somebody's loved one will end up in heaven unless there's actual proof. Only thing is, I hope there is a heaven. If I knew for certain there was, I'd work harder at trying to unravel the mystery of how you get there.

On the way from the guesthouse the morning after I arrived in Transylvania, I'd asked Aunt Vivian her thoughts on heaven and vampires, this business of drinking the blood of Christ at communion.

"I wasn't much older than you when I became a Christian," she told me. "It was something you did back then. All the girls my age went to church. Most of the boys, too. Except for David Ashworth. He was sorry trash and ended up in prison."

"I don't know hardly any boys my age who go to church," I'd replied. "The kids I know aren't interested in religion."

"Christianity isn't a religion, dear. Religion is full of rules and penalties."

"But if I don't believe like you, I go to hell, don't I? That sounds like a seriously big rule to me."

Aunt Vivian smiled at me, reached over, and patted my arm. "I'll pray God speaks to your heart. That's the only way you ever come to him anyway. He has to call you."

The minister motioned for us to sit. Tissues appeared. He opened a Bible and began.

"Joy comes in the morning. Weeping may endure for a night, but joy comes in the morning. I pray it is so. I pray the merciful God in heaven ..."

I tuned out his words. There was nothing he could say that would help. Edwards, that monster ... there was nothing the minister could add or subtract that would undo what had happened. I allowed my mind to replay those final moments with Lieutenant McAlhany.

Edwards did not drive Aunt Vivian's car to the morgue as I'd expected. Another miscalculation by the "know-it-all Nick Caden." Instead he'd driven Meg to a hunting cabin. We'd turned into the dirt drive and McAlhany had parked about a quarter mile from the cabin. From there we hiked in. The lieutenant had asked me to wait at the edge of the clearing while he approached the cabin. Aunt Vivian's car was parked beside the house. I stood close enough to hear the engine pinging and popping as it cooled. From behind a tree I'd watched McAlhany edge over to a side window. Standing on tiptoes he'd peered in, then nodded to me to let me know they were inside. The plan was for me to run back to the squad car and confirm we had located the suspect, but before I could...

"But every time we think we have reached our capacity to face our fears, we are reminded that our ability to confront evil will be limitless. This is a time for remembering the God of love who looks not upon our weakness and turns away, but the

God of love who understands our brokenness and extends his strong arm of grace and mercy. Through God's love in Christ we are ..."

But I hadn't run back to the squad car. Instead I'd watched as McAlhany unholstered his revolver and brought it up. Sirens sang and flashing blue lights appeared through the trees as more police cars arrived.

Suddenly corner floodlights winked on. The side yard became a dome of yellow. The full-throated blast of a shotgun created a football-sized hole in the cabin's clapboard siding. McAlhany staggered backward and turned toward me, his lips pulled back away from his teeth, face twisted in agony. He dropped to his knees and fell forward with his right arm folded across his gut. In the spill of blood pooling underneath him, he aimed his eyes at me and tried to smile.

Law officers rushed to the building, surrounding it. My gaze remained on McAlhany, even as Meg's frantic screams rose above the *blam-blam* of gunfire.

" ... so today we remember not just our friend, but a hero, Lieutenant Ralph McAlhany, a servant of Christ."

"It's not your fault," I heard Meg say. Her words sounded far, far away, like the wispy sounds of a breeze building in the forest. *"You couldn't have done anything; it's not your fault."*

Tears stung my eyes. The minister droned on. I sniffed and wiped my nose on the cuff of my shirtsleeve.

Meg's arm slipped from its sling. She rested her hand atop mine and squeezed.

"It's not your fault," she said softly. "Really, it's not. Let it go, Nick. You have to let it go."

Comforted by her words, I closed my eyes and breathed in deep. Exhaling, I felt a weight lift from my shoulders. I knew the lieutenant's death would haunt me forever, but I couldn't change the past. I couldn't fix my mistakes. I'd been too sure of myself, too cocky, and now he was dead. But still, there are things that are simply out of our control, and death is one of them. If nothing else, all this nonsense with vampires had proven that.

The prayer ended. I opened my eyes and watched Meg's sad eyes moisten. The pastor worked his way down the row, whispering comforting words to the lieutenant's family. Still clutching Meg's hand, I stood and pulled her toward the casket.

If there is a God in heaven, I hope he judges us by our acts of bravery, not by our cowardly thoughts. I don't know what dark secrets Lieutenant Ralph McAlhany had squirreled away, what hidden sins he harbored in his heart. If Aunt Vivian is right about all this God and Jesus business, it only matters that the lieutenant was man enough to admit he needed help, that he couldn't save himself. I hope he owned up to his shortcomings and, in those final moments before he breathed his last, asked God for help.

I've been thinking maybe I should ask for help too.

I placed my corsage on the casket.

"He would want you to write this story," Meg said, pulling me away. "Come on, you can borrow my laptop. I'll help you get started."

CHAPTER EIGHTEEN
SUGAR CAKES

On a crisp autumn afternoon we gathered in Aunt Vivian's house to go through her things. Old cookie cutter tins, boxes of knitting yarn, drawers and drawers of dress patterns.

Meg sat on the bed riffling through one of Aunt Vivian's old photo albums. "Is that your dad?"

I leaned over Meg's shoulder and looked at the picture. "Yeah. No wonder *I* needed braces. I inherited Dad's beaver teeth."

"That's the last of it," Mom said, walking into the den. "Your father has the Cadillac loaded down. We'll put the rest in storage."

"You most certainly will not. It's coming with me."

Mom winked at me and, turning toward Aunt Vivian, said, "We've been over this already. You cannot put everything you own in that tiny apartment; there isn't enough room."

"Hon, I'm not taking everything, just the important stuff. You'll help me, right, Nick?"

"Absolutely. Whatever you say, Aunt Vivian."

After her heart attack, she agreed it would be best if she moved into the assisted living complex, but being Aunt Vivian, she insisted on setting the terms of the move.

I said, "And anytime you want to go to the storage unit, let me know and I'll drive you there."

"Lord, child, I'm not going to ask you to drive all that way from Kansas just for that. Why, that's the most foolish thing I've ever heard."

"Aunt Vivian, by the time you get around to missing this stuff, I'll have my permit. I'll need the practice, right, Mom?"

"We'll talk about it later."

"Bless you, dear, but I couldn't."

"Come on," I said, walking Aunt Vivian out of the room and toward the kitchen. "You promised me a batch of sugar cakes."

"Oh, Nick, I am so going to miss having you around."

"I'm not gone yet. We don't leave until tomorrow. I still have to run by Raintree's bookstore and apologize to him and Barlow for thinking they were involved in Forester's death. I guess in some ways I feel responsible for putting the vampire slayer game out of business."

"Don't waste your time," said Meg. "Raintree sold the store and is in the midst of setting up that nature conservancy. The store's new owner read about the vampire murder, flew down, and made an offer the week after you left. And Barlow, oh wow, did he ever catch a break. One of the producers of that television show *Kill Me Now* contacted him about becoming a regular on the show. Wouldn't have happened if not for your article. So in one sense your poking around in Forester's death was a blessing for both."

"Just the same, I'm coming back to visit. I promise."

"Don't make promises you can't keep," Meg said.

"We're not going there again, are we?" I said, trying to hide my smile.

"Just saying, the last time you promised someone ..."

"Look at you two, arguing like an old married couple. Come on, let's head over to my new apartment before I forget how to drive."

"Shotgun!" I yelled.

"Fine. But you have to make sure she stays on the road," Meg said, punching me on the arm.

From the foyer Aunt Vivian called, "Has anyone seen my wallet? I know I had it a second ago."

I caught Meg's eye, winked, and said to Aunt Vivian, "Is that it under your arm?"

"Oh, Nick, whatever will I do when you're not around?"

Dear Cool Ghoul readers: I'm writing this on my new tablet from the backseat of our car. We're on our way back to Kansas. One final thought as I close the file on the Forester case. I still don't know who mugged me in the alley. Edwards still insists it wasn't him. I believe him. Maybe it was someone pretending to be a vampire. Or one of the lieutenant's men trying to discourage me from meddling in the case. Could be I'll never know. But I have a hunch I'll face that phantom again.

And soon.

FOR FURTHER INVESTIGATION

Questions written by Sarah Lynn Phillips

1. Nick's dad encourages him to visit Aunt Vivian and makes this statement: "Family is everything." Do you agree or disagree? Why or why not? How did Nick's opinion of his great-aunt and the importance of family change? Why did he refer to her as "a Golden Globe–winning aunt"?

2. Nick unearthed legends, myths, stories, and alleged history about vampires. His discoveries led him to suppose people's belief in them "isn't all that new." What's your take on the lieutenant's conclusion? "Only proves people today who believe in vampires aren't any smarter today than they were back then."

3. The note signed by Barnabas Forester read, "Fear the darkness, for it is in the black hearts of men that evil lurks ... Take my warning seriously ... Escape now while you still can, for if you do not, you too may find yourself forever bound by the curse of darkness." How does this warning compare with the teachings of Jesus found in the Bible? Investigate the following:

   - Jeremiah 17:9

   - Matthew 15:17–20

   - Mark 7:21

   - Romans 1:21

4. Aunt Vivian said, "We make time for the things that matter." Nick's father *said* family mattered, but his busyness prevented him from visiting his aunt. What things matter enough to you so that you make time for them? What do you *say* is important but your actions show otherwise?

5. What do you think Aunt Vivian meant when she quoted Jesus from Matthew 10:16, "Be wise as serpents and harmless as doves"? Do you think she bribed the doctor by paying him to let Nick see the body, or did her action demonstrate shrewdness? Why?

6. Forester's widow said, "Seeing how the rest of the world lives really makes you appreciate where you're from [and] ... what you have." Do you think this is true? Can you recall a time when you or someone you know visited a third-world country? How was that person changed as a result?

7. The phantom figure in the room of caskets asks Nick, "Do you believe a person can gain eternal life through the blood of another?" How would *you* answer this question? Compare your response to the clues written on ancient scrolls two thousand years ago:

   • Romans 5:8–9

   • Hebrews 9:22

   • 1 John 1:7

8. Consider the age-old quest for immortality. Is it possible for a human to be immortal (Hebrews 9:27)? How do mortal people gain eternal life? How would you assist Nick in his quest "to unravel the mystery" and live forever? Take a close-up look at John 3:16 and Ephesians 2:4–9.

9. Aunt Vivian asserted, "Where I'm going they pave the streets with gold." Examine Revelation 21:21 to see why she seemed so confident. Take a virtual tour of Heaven by investigating Revelation 21:1–5, 15–27, and 22:1–5. If you knew with certainty there was life after death, how would that change your view of your present problems?

10. Nick knew he couldn't change the past, fix his mistakes, or save himself. He realized some things, such as death, were out of his control. Where would you advise Nick to seek help? How do Matthew 7:7–8 and Hebrews 4:16 relate to Nick's new attitude?

Talk It Up!

Want free books?
First looks at the best new fiction?
Awesome exclusive merchandise?

We want to hear from you!

Give us your opinions on titles, covers, and stories.
Join the Z Street Team.

Email us at zstreetteam@zondervan.com
to sign up today!

Also—Friend us on Facebook!

www.facebook.com/goodteenreads

- Video Trailers
- Connect with your favorite authors
- Sneak peeks at new releases
- Giveaways
- Fun discussions
- And much more!